DeathWatch

Lisa Mannetti

PRAISE FOR DEATHWATCH

"Lisa Mannetti's Deathwatch is horror at its most intelligent and subtle. These two tales delve deep into ghastly subjects as varied as the butcher shop history of early modern surgery and criminal madness and demonic rape, and yet Lisa Mannetti writes with such compassion for her characters that even their horrific lives seem sympathetic. And, AND, she does it with prose so finely crafted and absorbing that I lost an entire evening somewhere in the pages of these tales. This is the kind of book that forms the foundation of a great literary career. Treat yourself to an evening with Lisa Mannetti. She's going to leave you breathless."

—**Joe McKinney**, Bram Stoker Award-winning author of DEAD CITY and APOCALYPSE OF THE DEAD

"In a genre glutted with soulless practitioners, grinding out "product" like sausages, Lisa Mannetti's continues to be a refreshingly personal voice. Her work is idiosyncratic, erudite, intense … and authentically nightmarish."

—**Robert Dunbar**, author of MARTYRS & MONSTERS and WILLY

"Lisa Mannetti presents two haunting tales that will resonate in your dreams long after you've put these novellas down. Mannetti's prose draws you in and holds you tight as she pulls you into the stories of Stuart Granville and Tom Smith. Haunting and intense, Deathwatch is a must-read for fans of Gothic horror and Mannetti's unique voice."

—**Teresa Frohock**, author of MISERERE: AN AUTUMN TALE (Night Shade Books, July 2011)

"If you miss out on Deathwatch, you're surely missing out on something special."

—**Colum McKnight**, *Paperback Horror*

For Dr. Steven Ross *in memoriam.*

You always believed in me.
I'll miss you, my friend.

SECRETS AWAIT
– An Introduction

Secrets.

    We all have them. We all keep them. Little girls in school whisper to one another, "I love Joe, but don't tell anybody!" Teen boys hide certain kinds of magazines in their rooms, ordering their friends to not say a word to another soul about them. College students promise not to let on that their roommates cheated on an exam. Wealthy ladies have secret clubs in which they shoplift cheap jewelry merely for the rush. CEO's enjoy clandestine, hush-hush trysts behind closed doors with their willing...or less than willing...underlings.

    Secrets. Some harmless and sweet. Others destructive, festering, and rooted in obsessions.

    The deepest, most obsessive secrets seem to be those kept in the bosom of the family. The family is the most intimate unit of humanity, and in such intimacy secrecy flourishes.

"Don't tell the neighbors."

"Don't tell your friends."

"Don't you dare tell anyone what you saw, what I said, what we did..."

Hoarders get away with their mental illnesses long enough for the piles to grow into hills, the hills into mountains, for pets to die and become fossilized beneath layers of magazines, trash, feces, broken furniture and broken dreams. It swells to monstrous proportions, leaving those inside crawling, clambering, tripping, falling, and sometimes even dying amid the mess.

Those with gambling addictions swear their wives, husbands, and children to secrecy even as finances spiral down the drain and the families, clutching and screaming silently, spin down with it.

Sexual predators thrive within the safe walls of family secrecy. Tiptoeing up the stairs, down the halls. Doors easing shut. Shh, don't let the bed squeak. Shh, don't tell your mother, she wouldn't understand.

So here we have Lisa Mannetti's *Deathwatch*. I didn't know what to expect when I began reading. I know Lisa is an incredible writer. And this collection once more confirms how brilliantly talented she is. The stories slammed me in the gut and heart; they ran up my spine and built horrible, twisted nests in my brain. With "Dissolution" and "Sheila Na Gig," Lisa peels back thick layers of familial secrets; she pries open locked shutters and forces wide the doors. She doesn't only offer us a peek inside but rather pushes us, head first, into nightmarish, claustrophobic worlds where families cling together even as they destroy one another. My first reaction was "Holy shit!" (pardon my French, and why French, I wonder? But I digress...) Then, "Oh, my God."

Both tales are set in the past, a past that seems to have no color, a past that seethes and hisses, that tastes of foods gone bad and smells of sicknesses uncured. The secrets in these stories, however, are not left in the past but are secrets of the ages, secrets that are way too close to our souls for comfort.

In "Dissolution," failed medical student Stuart Granville has no idea what he is stumbling into when he accepts a position in New York to teach twin girls. Girls whom, he discovers upon his arrival, are conjoined, and their physician father wants help taking them apart. Now, if you're anything like me, medical practices from the 19th century give me the willies. And that's just for starters. There is a force at play inside the dark and foreboding household, a force that savors secrets and the obsessions and power they create.

In "Sheila Na Gig," young Irishman Tom Smith is trapped in the web of his family's obsessions. With a foul witch for a grandmother (one of the most dreadful and perfectly created characters I've read in a long time), he struggles to cling to love, maintain sanity, and seek his freedom in spite of the web of secrets that threaten to drown him.

When I shut this book I was shuddering. I had been there with Stuart and Tom. I had struggled, agonized, and screamed with them. Lisa's skillful research into the time and place of these stories, her ability to describe just the right item, just the right scent, just the right flickering of tainted light through a window or squeal of the floor beneath a boot heel, makes *Deathwatch* a complete experience. And while it is complete and wonderfully literate as it is, I can easily imagine this on the silver screen. Come on, filmmakers out there. This is intelligent horror. This is what our genre is all about.

- Elizabeth Massie

*—Last night I heard the deathwatch
ticking in the wall—*

—Oliver Goldsmith

DISSOLUTION

1

I was twenty when I first came to Hyde Park, New York and fell in love with the child who was both woman and ghost. And God help me, it was my infatuation—or obsession—if you prefer, that spawned both her strange shadow life as my bride and—later, much later—her death.

It was December, and the Hudson River was frozen. I hailed from the Carolinas, and after a bleak train ride north, my first, my strongest memory of the region was that solid white mass like a road, of wind blowing and the sight of tight-lipped red faced men hauling blocks of ice on sledges, the horses straining for purchase on the slippery surface.

Their shouts were muffled by the heavy, quiet fall of snow, even the sound of the train whistling as it left the depot was deadened, and standing on the wooden platform, the chill of the boards penetrating my thin-soled shoes, I thought, I have come to a lonely place. White and cold and deathly still.

Andrew Saunders sent his hired man to meet me. He spotted me right off: I was the only fool not swathed to the eyebrows in heavy wool.

"Mr. Granville." He raised an eyebrow, but there was no question in his tone of voice. He put out a thick-gloved hand. "Gabriel Wickstrom," he said. "The doctor asked me to fetch you."

"I suppose you are an angel—rescuing me in this bitter cold."

He grunted. "You'll get used to it. Carriage is this way." He'd taken the smaller of my two bags, and I followed him down a rickety flight of stairs; his shoulders were covered with a small drift of wet melting snow, and I wondered if he'd waited a long time for me, if perhaps the cold made him so businesslike and terse.

He heaved the bag into the floorspace of a winter-converted two wheel buggy. "There's a footwarmer—if the coals haven't gone out," he advised when I climbed in. He handed me a furry lap robe and I snuggled under it. Gabriel plied the whip lightly, and the horse picked up its pace jogging through the snowy streets.

"Heard the doc got you cheap, because you were sent down, is that so?" he asked.

"Yes," I said, vaguely aware there was a something like a glint of humor in his eye. My parents had sent me to the University of Virginia, but I'd been expelled for drinking. "Yes, they gave me the boot, all right. There's a chance they may re-admit me next fall."

"You'll stay sober enough, likely. The doctor had my Missus—Ruth she's called—clear out every drop in the house. Or as good as. The stuff's locked up tighter than a virgin's cooze in a great big cabinet down cellar. She has the keys."

I nodded.

"A man needs a drink now and then," he said, his dark eyes staring ahead through the swirling snow. "You see me if you get to feeling that way."

"I suppose the doctor will be asked to give an account of me at year's end before the university will take me back." I held my hands up. "I'm good at what I do, you know. I like

16

surgery. Even if I'm only the children's tutor, it was luck that found me this place. At least I'll be around a doctor, I can read his textbooks, keep up with things—"

"Tutor?"

"Yes, for the girls, Abby and Eleanor."

"I think he has more in mind than that—"

"What do you mean?"

"Nothing. Except he only wrote to medical colleges...." Gabriel tucked his chin deep inside his collar. "You know they're twins?"

"Yes. And according to what Dr. Saunders said, they've fallen behind in their studies. Other girls going on twelve speak French and have at least a smattering of Latin—"

He made a sound like a snort.

"What's so funny?"

"Fallen behind. That sounds like they've had any education at all—but he never could keep a teacher more than a month or two at most."

I looked around thinking the place was isolated, but there were good-sized towns. Poughkeepsie was actually a small city, there would be several schools to choose from.

He seemed to read my thoughts. "Never been to school, none hereabouts would have 'em."

"What! Why not? Two girls couldn't possibly get up to that much mischief."

"Give the other kids the willies—the teachers too. Then the boys and girls go to making fun, and Abby and Eleanor cry—well you can't blame 'em for that." He turned to me, and it was just that moment that the gaslights were going on here and there—like yellow beacons with haloes in the snow. "You don't know, do you?"

I shook my head.

"Abby and Ellie, they was born stuck together. Siamese Twins, the doctor calls 'em. Like those oriental freaks they sport in a circus."

"Are they...." The question died on my lips, because I had a hundred questions. Where was the jointure? Were they expected to live? Could they walk?

"Their ma's dead," he said abruptly. "Dr. Saunders, maybe he went a little crazy. Grief does strange things to a man. I know. Mrs. Ruth and me, the way we see it, his idea— it's like Solomon's notion, taking a child and splitting it in two—"

"He means to separate them?"

"He hired you. A surgeon, like you said," he leaned out. "Good with your hands," he finished; then spit over the side. "Ho, Bessie," he soothed, reining the horse. "No more palaver now, we're here."

The house, a large rambling mass as tall and white as an iceberg, loomed out at me across a long spread of snow-covered lawn, and I felt my stomach clench. My hands, under the warm blanket, twitched, and I was suddenly cold.

"Fly Abby, let's fly!"

Gabriel Wickstrom and I had entered a dimly lit large slate-floored hallway, stamping our feet free of snow; above our heads in what I guessed was the twin of the space we were standing in, I heard the clattering sound of metal wheels rolling on wooden planks, the high pitched squeal of giggling glee.

"Fly, Fly!"

"It's the girls," Gabriel said, his eyes flicking up toward the white plastered ceiling. There was a soft bumping noise; the hollow echoing ratchet of the wheels turning round and round like a cheap carnival ride. "A kind of jerry-rigged contraption," he said. "A toy sheep. I made it myself— children got to run, best they can—"

The sound of two doors opening cut him off. From the upper one came a woman's sharp voice, telling the girls to leave off their play and go down to meet their new teacher. From the lower one—a large paneled mahogany slab that led to what looked like the library—a tall stiff man in a black cutaway coat emerged, clearing his throat. Dr. Saunders had a pair of gray eyes he kept averted from mine. When he shook my hand and introduced himself, I caught the sharp musk of sherry on his breath.

"Ah, my daughters." He turned abruptly.

At the far end of the dreary entryway, I saw a small gated niche I'd overlooked. From its rising throat I heard the screak of hemp ropes, the drop-and-settle-drop-and-settle of a wooden platform moving through metal channels.

"Elevator," Gabriel hissed, scuttling quickly to throw back the gate and seize a pair of ropes. "Harder to manage from above with the weight," he said, peering up inside the darkened recess. "Got, em Ruth," he called. Whatever she said was lost in the thump-slide of the cage moving down the shaft.

The platform bumped to floor level. Gabriel wound, then knotted the ropes around a heavy cleat set into the wall. He opened the metal door of the cage.

And I had my first glimpse of the twins.

They stood, smiling, their arms locked around each other's waists. They looked for all the world like any two young girls sharing a moment of sweet embrace. Except, my eyes had grown used to the dim gas light, and now I picked out the startling details: the single-bodiced frock with its lumps and swatches of fabric that could not be sewn smooth, the drift of green velvet skirt below as wide as the cloth for a pasha's table.

They began limp-walking toward me like children hobbling in a three-legged race at a summer picnic. But there was no giggling at the awkwardness, no shrieks of laughter. They moved slowly, somberly, and I understood at once—the

19

old pictures from my medical texts flashing up at me—the jointure was at the hip.

2

Dinner was a nightmare. Andrew Saunders got drunk; I was not even offered a sip. In between courses in the drafty dining room the girls stared at me—harder, I'm sure, than anyone might ever have had nerve enough to stare at them. Ruth and Gabriel served— they were obviously unused to company; they twittered and fussed, never doing anything that was to the doctor's satisfaction.

"The roast's cold. Where's the soufflé I ordered?"

Ruth, a tall woman, stood by the side board wringing a pair of outsized hands, her eyes nervously darting over the room.

"Sorry, Doctor. You were so long with the first course, I wasn't sure of the timing. It's the wind tonight, blowing right through the windows of the pantry—"

He grunted, standing over the beef, the carving knife and fork trembling in his hands. He had just used his fingers to tweeze a large slab of meat onto the serving platter. No one commented. I looked away.

She went on. "I kept it covered with the silver dome, the wind has a way of going right through these old walls on a winter night." She began to go around the table with a bowl of new potatoes, holding the china at the shoulder level for each of us in turn.

I watched Abby and Ellie. They were seated on a raised bench like a piano stool. Ellie forked potatoes efficiently onto her plate; Abby was forced to use her left hand and she was not so dexterous. A buttered round skidded onto the polished surface.

Ruth retrieved it quickly, wiped the table with her apron hem, and covered the girl's embarrassment: "The soufflé is still in the oven, Sir."

"Well see that it's served hot. What are you two staring at?" He flung his napkin down.

"Nothing," Ellie said.

Abby flicked her gaze toward her father. He was pre-occupied, pouring what must have been his sixth or seventh glass of wine. He drained it, poured another; then he lowered his grizzled head like some blind old ox foraging in its manger and began to eat.

"We don't see many people," Abby said quietly, looking into my eyes. Her hair—like her sister's—was sheened red and glossy in the lamplight. It was done in a puff of ringlets, and I spotted more of Ruth's handiwork.

"Some from the nursery window," Ellie added. "The butcher's boy. Abby has a crush on *him*," she giggled.

"Quiet. Mr. Granville doesn't want to hear your truck and nonsense," Abby said. "We heard you're a doctor, we're most anxious to have our surgery done," she said.

That remark, spoken in a very low voice, roused the doctor.

"Get out, get out the pair of you! Sneaking spies, always lurking about, listening, watching. I said out! Get out this minute."

Ellie turned white, but Abby whispered at me. "Excuse us. It's the drink you know. Ever since mother—"

"Ruth," he yelled, "get these vixens out of the dining room—"

She hurried in, helping them off the bench, lending her arm for support, then steering them toward the door. I heard it shut abruptly, and then through the adjoining wall, the rattle of the metal cage, the squeak-rub of the ropes being hoisted, the platform groaning its way toward the second floor.

"Poor things," I said.

"Yes. We're all of us poor things in this house. They say that God helps those who help themselves. But I've been crushed by my own life. First them, the damnable freak birth, the years of watching them grow twisted and maimed while idiots' children run like jackrabbits. And then my wife, the only human being I ever loved. She killed herself, you know."

In the silence that followed, the doctor fixed his gray eyes on me, and I saw they'd gone silver cloudy, not just with drink, but from bone-deep cynicism. The man was in pain. Half-startled, I pushed away from the table, Abby's words ringing in my mind: It's the drink. Ever since mother died, he drinks to shut us out, to shut himself down.

She was a month shy of twelve years old, and she had just taught me my first lesson.

3

"**I**t's snowing." Abby's voice held a note of joyous expectation. She clapped her hands. "It's the perfect birthday gift!"

It was just past dawn on the morning of February 12. The girls stood, their backs to me, peering out the high, wide mullioned window of the nursery.

"Aren't you scared, Abby?" Ellie squeezed her sister's hand.

"No, and no! It's freedom, Ellie!" She started the first steps of a pirouette, pulling her sister with her. Her white nightdress fanned and rose in a circle.

I had risen early—with just as much anticipation—and now I rapped my knuckles against the wooden jamb of the open nursery door. They turned toward me, I saw the color rising in their young faces, and something turned inside me.

Abby's dark blue eyes were shining.

"It's the best gift, the best birthday present in the world," she said softly. "After the surgery, we'll be like other girls. We can dream their dreams, we'll be free to dream. We never could do that before, Mr. Granville."

From below, I caught the sharp scent of carbolic acid, the pungency of alcohol and ether. There was a faint clink of steel instruments being laid out in the office the doctor kept here at home, and I willed myself not to look at my hands.

25

"I'm scared, Abby," Ellie whispered, and I saw the muscles of her jaw tense. "What if we die?"

Abby shook her head, took her twin's right hand between both of hers. "Don't be." Her hands found their way to her sister's forehead, and she smoothed her hair and temples, looking for all the world like a mother comforting a child with the reassurance love brings. "Ellie, when we go downstairs, it's the last time we go as freaks—"

"You're not a freak, Abby. I love you."

It was very true. I felt the same myself. I felt all three of us were sleepwalking over a cliff in some strange dream. All the same, I helped them onto the elevator, lowering the platform, steadying the ropes until Gabriel took over from below. Then I walked slowly down the wide stairway, and met the doctor in his office.

He'd wheeled the dining room table in to accommodate their bulk; but two separate iron beds lay pushed against the far wall of the room. It took the three of us—Gabriel, the doctor and myself—to lift the girls onto the sheet-covered makeshift operating table. Overhead, a bright lamp threw its harsh glare on the girls' pale, upturned faces. Abby put her hand out, and I took it, clumsily patting her shoulder at the same time. Dr. Saunders frowned at me.

"Pull yourself together, Granville. They're my children, after all."

I nodded. Gabriel was looking very white. He kept licking his lips, and I knew he was nearly desperate for a cigarette or a drink—or both. "You don't have to watch the actual surgery," I said, "just hand us what we need, when we need it."

"Right." He nodded, I turned to look at the instruments one last time, the descriptions I'd pored and sweated over the last month rolling through my head. I began to focus, to breathe a little deeper and easier.

"Ready?"

"Yes," I slipped a white gauze mask over my mouth and nose, and used a sterilized ice pick to open the first can of ether. It made a little plock—the sound of air rushing in— then hissed when I opened a second vent. I saturated a thick wad of cloth and pressed it gently against Abby's mouth and nose.

"Just breathe normally."

"We're twins," she giggled, rolling her eyes toward my own white swath of mask.

Saunders had upended the open can, and was likewise giving Ellie anesthesia.

"Fly, Abby, let's fly," she whispered just before her head swiveled bonelessly sideways and she lost consciousness.

I saw Gabriel make the sign of the cross.

It was as brilliant a surgery as any I'd seen before—or since. Saunders was in high glee. He'd guessed that the jointure was not profound, and when he opened them up and saw with his own eyes that the pelvic bones were like the bottoms of two tea-cups end to end with a small lumpy bridge between them, he whooped.

"Piece of cake," he said.

They did share one loop of intestine, but we cut and tied it quickly. There were no annoying tiny vessels presenting as bleeders. When I took off a clamp after he sutured, the stitches held.

Gabriel winced and squinched his eyes at the sound of the bone saw; for me it was a miracle. For the first time the girls were separate, two beings unlocked from the grotesquerie of their birth.

"Christ," I whispered under my breath.

"You see," Saunders said, "now they're older, they've got their growth, we can reshape the bone—both of them will walk normally. I've waited all these years for this day, Granville. I've heard of doctors in Europe doing this to younger children. Almost always one of them ends up with a crippling malformation. They can't predict the growth pattern of the bones."

"Someday, I suppose," I said.

"Yes, in fifty or a hundred years if they can re-configure the microscope, otherwise a man's just going in and groping blind." He paused. "You close Abby, I'll do Eleanor," he said, and I found myself sneaking looks and watching to see how he tucked and stretched the skin.

"Mind the scar."

I could see his grin behind the mask; he went on, "I believe our Abby's going to be a vain girl—and well she should—with a face like hers."

It was the first time I thought about the twins that way, and I saw it was not just a father's love, he was right. They had dark blue eyes, fine spun reddish hair. Their mouths were cherub's pouts. They were pretty.

"We're pioneers," I said. This was slow, careful work, but not more difficult than what a good seamstress could do.

"There've not been more than a handful of successful separations. 'Course, it's not like they were buried one inside the other's chest, like some I've seen. Or those cases where the children lie head to head—like human pinwheels."

I twitched at the words, the needle caught in the girl's scant flesh. Abby moaned in her sleep.

"Give her just a touch more ether," Saunders said casually—one colleague to another—and I marveled at this second miracle: if the girls were separate, he and I, by virtue of our work were joined.

4

Saunders had left me to go dose himself with the first drink he'd taken in a week; so I sat alone waiting in the cool of the darkened room, keeping vigil while the girls slept off the anesthesia. There wasn't much to do; I checked their pulses often, watched the color slowly returning to their waxy faces. Twice Abby moaned lightly, and Eleanor's hands twitched in a dry rasp against the coverlet, startling me briefly while I brooded on the peculiar life I'd led during the past month.

I'd expected to do a sort of penance to make up for being expelled—had, in fact, exiled myself to a low status job in a place that was far from home and friends. But I hadn't been prepared for the sheer isolation that made me feel I was living in a sort of ghost house—a microcosmic Brigadoon—that appeared or vanished at will.

The doctor had no patients—or none that I ever saw. Each morning as we were finishing breakfast and the hall clock chimed nine, he consulted his pocket watch, replaced it in his black wool vest, then clumped down the hallway to his office. I don't know what he did there. Occasionally he left the house, his medical bag in hand and said he was going out on a house call. But there were none of the flurried knocks in the middle of the night, anxious voices asking for care, or medicines; no sickly wailing babies soothed by worried mothers, none of the constant activity I associated with a doctor's busy practice.

Apart from delivery boys, there were no visitors either. The first week, I assumed the heavy brooding weather kept the doctor's friends from dropping by. But by the end of the month, no one had come. When I looked out the window at the frozen landscape, the fantastically whittled drifts and blowing snow, I felt as if the rest of the world outside the house had suddenly come to a stop.

That was outside; inside I felt something that was equally stifling. Routines are often soothing, they allow life to mesh neatly. But in Saunders's house, they were like the strong silky threads of a spider web: nearly invisible, but capable of holding a man mute, fast.

Mornings, I tried to teach Abby and Ellie the rudiments. They were bright enough; but their deformity got in the way. They sat on a bench, like those in any country schoolroom, but forced to use one hand, their papers flew from the desktop.

"Stuart," one or the other would announce, after I'd set them to writing compositions or doing a raft of sums. I'd look up from Saunders's grimy anatomy book and meet two pairs of eyes.

It was easier for me to get up and retrieve the yellow lined paper than it was for them. I thought I'd solved the problem by fixing the pages down with small balls of wax. But there would be a brief silence followed by the tapping sound of pencils bouncing on the floor, and once, a gasp when Abby upset a jar of ink over both of them.

We tried oral lessons and reading aloud. I took to using a blackboard.

"Now, repeat after me," I'd say, hearing Ruth's scrape outside the door, or the doctor's cough.

They wouldn't though. They only peered up at me, small wry smiles on their faces. Sometimes one or the other asked a question:

"Were you ever in love?"

"Do you like us?"

I ignored these questions, but the sound of my own voice droning geography lessons and Latin verbs made me feel like I was living in a vacuum. I guessed the school work bored them—they made so many slow halting trips to the bathroom—and of course, if one went to squat over the double seated box of a 'toilet' Gabriel had built, her twin had no choice but to sit dangling her legs over the other chamber pot concealed in the cabinet.

In the evenings I sat in the library poring over surgical literature and looking at sketches and drawings and reading the doctor's notes. Overhead, I'd hear the sound of the wheels of their toy sheep turning hollowly against the floor boards. Saunders had forbidden them to cry out while I studied, and their unnatural silence made it all the eerier. And that thin noise began to haunt my sleep and invade the quiet time with my books. My head would jerk up from my work at the sound of the metal wheels ratcheting along, the small bump when the stuffed animal tipped against the window seat which had been covered in a strip of old carpeting. Stifled giggles, whispers. Then at eight o'clock, Ruth would ready them for bed. The sameness of it all grated on me, and from downstairs I could have set my watch by the little sounds from the nursery. Ruth drawing the drapes and bringing the girls cups of chocolate, the spoons clinking against the china. The final trip to the bathroom, and then my name called lightly on the chill air of the house.

"Stuart...we're ready."

At the sound, the doctor, half drunk, would pop like a jack in the box out of his office, his face red, his collar hanging like a tiny flag, and eye me up and down.

"They're calling you, Granville. Go on up. Why else am I paying you?" And he would reel away toward the cellar—or if he was too unsteady, bellow for Gabriel to fetch him another bottle.

Saunders had conceived the idea that I should be the one to read them a bedtime story, so I would tuck a book under my arm and go up to that room, the fire sunk down to a pale strip of orange light on the hearth, the shadowy faces of the girls lying on their bed, propped with pillows. What Saunders never knew was that my book was window-dressing. When I climbed the stairs each night, it was the girls who spun the tales; Ruth banished, their voices a dark whisper.

"Mother is here again, you know," Ellie said. I'd been there just a little more than a week. Outside, the January snow spat against the windows, closing us all in.

"Her name is Regina," Abby added. "Regina Cahill, before she became Saunders."

"She comes in our dreams."

I was sitting on a low, red leather hassock alongside the bed, my hands limp between my upraised knees. The girls peered down at me, and suddenly I felt absurdly small.

"Do you have the same dream?" I asked.

"Not at all," Ellie shook her head. "It's better that way, don't you think?" She paused, picking at the coverlet. "She likes you. She wants the surgery soon—"

"Ssh," Abby punched her sister lightly. "She killed herself, and now we know why. I dreamed it." Her blue eyes were very bright. Then she closed them as if she'd gone back inside her dream and was searching for the details.

"After we were born, Father didn't want her. No he didn't," she said. Her voice was sad, mournful. "Mother understood. He was afraid there'd be more babies like us or worse."

I jumped. This was nothing a twelve year old—a completely sheltered twelve year old—could know, I thought.

"It was a long time, years and years, and her heart was full, but there was no one to love."

Her voice had the sound of a recitation, and it unnerved me. I stared at her, and for a second she seemed so much older than the ringleted child lying on the pillow, her ballerina doll with dripping, flesh-pink cloth legs cuddled in her arm.

"It was one of our teachers," Ellie put in, excitedly. "John Price—he was older than you—nearer our Mama's age.

Almost thirty-five. He was good looking. But not as handsome as you."

"He found out," Abby said, her eyes remote, hazy as a sleepwalker's in the dim lamplight.

"Andrew," I breathed. "He killed her...."

"No. She was quick with John's child," Ellie said. "It was a terrible time, a time of confusion. Part of her singing to the sleeping child within, most of her terrified, knowing the doctor's eye was sharp. She meant to go away to have it, and to keep it safe. She told herself knowing it lived—somewhere—would be enough."

Abby clutched the doll more tightly, her voice tinged with the same unearthly tone. "A drug in the tea...he knew, you see. He noticed she'd stopped taking wine with dinner. Mother felt his arms around her, lifting her while she slept heavy-headed as an opium eater. She felt him carrying her bulk down and down and into the office. One light glowed.

"'No Regina,' he whispered, 'No more monsters.' And then Mother felt the hard metal of the curette inserting itself like a cold snake between her legs. It was gone. He cut the baby out, limb by limb and bit by bit."

"Dear god," I said. Was this the source of the man's desperation?

Abby went on, her whispery voice overriding mine. "He sent John away. After that there were only lady teachers. He said he forgave Mother's infidelity, and yet, there it was between them. Always. It was in his eyes, and he wouldn't touch her. He drank more and more. He went to one of those low women, someone in an alley. She was drunk, too, when he put it up her, banging her against some broken down alley fence. He taunted Mother with it, 'I had a whore' he shrieked." Abby paused, and I saw her tongue creep out to lick her lips.

"Mother found him in bed with the last governess. The girl was wearing one of her own soft blue satin gowns, ripped down the center, the halves lying like jagged wings against the white sheets. She knew she'd never shut out the hideous picture: Andrew's mouth fastened on the girl's ruby-tipped breast, his fingers plunged between her naked white legs, her hands burrowing against his back, her voice a low scream.

"'Am I to have nothing?' Mother bristled. 'Nothing and no one?' Her stomach was in a knot, her mind whirling. The girl sat up, clutching the sheet to her breasts—but not before Mother saw the sheen of the moisture on her full thighs and the bold light in her eyes.

"'Get out, Regina,' Andrew said. 'Women who make monsters are not wanted here.'

"The girl tittered, and Mother fled.

"It would only get worse, she told herself. She was a prisoner here, condemned to a loveless life, forced to watch him flaunt his lust for others. He would not let her love anyone—even him. Mother knew there were drugs in the locked medicine cabinet, she didn't care if it was quick or slow or easy or painful. She latched the outer door of the office and went in; then she broke the glass pane on the closet door with her fist and took the first thing that came to her hand. Inside the small brown vial there was a white powder, sparkling crystals. She spilled it into her palm, and she began to eat." Abby stopped.

"She's here right now," Ellie said. "She comes to us at night. Can't you smell her?" She wrinkled her nose, sniffing.

I caught a faint perfume: Parma violets. My eyes were dragged to the bedclothes, I knew Ruth scented the cupboards with lavender.

"Violets," Ellie whispered. "The first scent of spring."

The air seemed suddenly drenched with warm rain, earth.

"When we're separated, they'll make our new clothes from hers," Abby said. I saw she was livelier, more alert. "She likes you, Stuart, the set of your shoulders, the way your eyes light. You don't smile enough—ah, but when you do."

I felt something brush my cheek, soft as fingertips trailing beloved flesh.

Ellie cocked her head. "She wants the surgery, sends him dreams to hurry. Ruth has been watering his wine, more and more. His hands will be steady, keep on with your work. She watches you."

I gave a small gasp, thinking back to times when I'd felt someone's keen stare while I turned the thin leaves of Saunders's heavy texts. Once the candle had gone out, and I'd heard the rustling sound of silk as if someone hurried from the room, wide skirts fluttering against the door jamb.

"You're her second chance. We're her salvation."

"Kiss us goodnight, Stuart," Abby said, and I leaned across the bed kissing each of their foreheads in turn. Abby's small arm went round my neck. She clung to me.

"Soon, Stuart," she whispered against my ear. I nodded thinking she meant the surgery.

"But only one of us can be chosen," Eleanor sad sadly. "Only one can survive...."

"Hush," I soothed, putting out the lamp. I left the nursery, the rational part of my mind saying it was nothing more than the fancies of two crippled girls, an imaginary game got up between them. Compensation it was called. Lonely, motherless, they invented her again. And lonely and friendless, isolated, I'd let them bewitch me with their half-truths and wishful thinking.

After that night, I made Ruth stay during the story hour. I didn't want to listen to or encourage their strange fantasies; but Abby and Ellie had no interest in my stories. I read tale after tale in Scheherezade; but I read to a pair of slack-faced dolls, their blank eyes upturned and fixed stonily on the white nursery ceiling. The only sound—apart from my thick voice—was the small, steady pricking of Ruth's needle—altering Regina's old gowns—in anticipation of their surgery.

"What is there to do or see hereabouts?" I asked the doctor one evening just before dinner. The month was dragging on. I felt the walls closing in; the silence was oppressive. It was just past five o'clock, he stood with his back to me looking past the library window at dead darkness. I sat in my usual place, a drift of papers and books under my nose, my eyes bleary from the dim light.

"Nothing," he said. He inhaled a small brown cigar, and I saw its glowing tip wink in the reflection of the glass. "I don't pay you to sightsee or carouse. I pay you to teach my daughters and bone up on surgical techniques."

"Am I your paid prisoner?" I said.

He stared back at me, his eyes hard. "What is there to do?" he mocked. "And don't bother asking Ruth or Gabriel. They won't answer."

He left abruptly, but not before he'd pulled another weighty volume—*A Textbook of Pathology*—from the shelves and slammed it on the flat of the mahogany desk.

I was no slave I told myself; it was only a question of waiting 'til he fogged out some night, snoring on a couch or in his bed. So, twice I ventured out in search of company, taking the doctor's carriage. The first time I drove north toward Rhinebeck, just inside the town limits I saw a white elephant of a place called the Beekman Arms Hotel, the oldest inn in America. Eagerly, I hitched the horse and sprinted up the brick walkway.

But it was dead winter, and apart from a few tight-lipped locals, there was no one to share an ale, or a joke with. I was a stranger, I was not stopping there, so the men talked around me in low voices and I felt walled off by their quick glances, by the way they turned back to their own cliques. I drank a brandy by the taproom fireplace. Northerners were narrow and suspicious, I thought. This wouldn't happen in the south. I stood up to go, paid my bill. I was going out the door when I caught the sound of the barkeep's quiet voice: "Lives in the house with the freaks. Teaches 'em."

"You can teach a two-headed cow to dance," another voice answered, "but that don't make it any prettier to look at."

I went out, wincing at the sound of soft, brittle laughter behind me. Earlier, the barkeep had asked me if I needed a room; I'd said no more than I lived nearby, that I was a tutor living with a doctor named Saunders. Stupid. I should have known better than to mention his name within 20 miles of the place.

The second time, I drove south toward Poughkeepsie determined to break the silent spell-like atmosphere of the house.

I cannot say what sent me back before I'd gone even two or three miles, unless it was the sight of the Roosevelt's house lit to the roofline, with a vast array of carriages entering, jockeying for spaces. There was obviously some huge party going on. I could see the dark silhouettes of figures moving up wide porch steps toward the doors. From across the frozen fields, I heard the distant sound of an orchestra, the violins clear and sweet.

Perhaps it was the thought of all those welcomed guests, people who knew one another as friends and lovers—and the contrast of my own loneliness. I lost heart, turned the horse around and returned feeling gloomier than when I'd left.

Now, I sat, watching the twins return to consciousness in the doctor's office. I felt a change coming. Certainly during the surgery, Saunders had been a different man—talkative, friendly. Perhaps the twins' deformity had been the thing that weighed all of them down, and their freedom would release him, too. With the thought, Saunders stepped lightly across the threshold, a bottle and two glasses in hand.

"It was good work, and good work calls for a celebration," he said, pouring. "Drink up, Stuart."

It was the first time he ever called me Stuart, and the wine was champagne—another first for me. I liked the giddy way it frothed inside the glass he handed me.

"Smooth," I said.

"As silk," he answered, and we both laughed, though I wasn't sure why. He called for more champagne and poured a round for Gabriel and Ruth, whose wide anxious eyes informed me they'd never seen the doctor in such a good humor.

We were both drunk and well into the fourth bottle when Ellie came to, her voice cutting like a scalpel through my champagne glaze.

"Pain," she screamed. "It hurts, it hurts, oh it hurts!" She struggled like a beached fish, and I saw the spasms take her. It was the after-effects of the ether; she began to gag.

Christ! She's vomiting, she'll drown! If she aspirates it, she'll die for sure, I thought, panic invading me. I banged the wine glass down, ignoring the sound of it shattering, and raced to her bedside. I rolled her to one side, thumped her back, then thrust my fingers deep inside her mouth to snatch at the slimy clots of vomitus, scraping my skin against her teeth.

Only one of us can survive

Her hollow words jumped in my mind.

"No," I shouted. "No! C'mon, Ellie, breathe, breathe!"

A greenish drool poured slowly from between her lips, there was no time to worry about a basin, I held her head and shoulders as best I could. Her stomach heaved—a welcome sight—and then she was merely sick, retching weakly over the side of the bed.

"Abby," she moaned. Her voice was a sob. I soothed her. Her sister was still asleep, Saunders had gone directly to her bed and was standing by.

Abby was blinking now; her hands swam around her head, but she showed no signs of throwing up. "Where am

40

I?" she muttered a second before she opened her eyes. "Where's Ellie?"

"Lost," Ellie said, and at the time I thought she was still disoriented from the anesthesia or from her near crisis. I didn't know it was the true beginning of the change I'd half sensed earlier, or that it was the antithesis—a rotting corpse—to the vibrant new life I'd imagined.

"I'm lost," Ellie mewled again.

Then they both faded out, drifting into the regular rhythms of deep, undrugged sleep.

5

Looking back, I suppose the change—Regina's ability to come through—was nearly immediate. I saw it, I'm not sure if Ruth did then. It was the second day the twins were post-op, and Ruth had gone in to give them sponge baths. They were still loggy, and I was waiting for her to finish in order to check their incisions. I was only half aware of the slosh of her washcloth dipping into the basin, the soft slur of the sheet as she slid out a languid arm or leg to clean it—

"I'm finished, Doctor," Ruth said. I felt a slight quickening—no one had ever called me doctor before—but I supposed I'd earned it, and I meant to play out the role by changing the girls' dressings with all the efficiency I could.

I went to Abby first, saw Ruth had dressed both her and Ellie in a pair of clean white nightgowns. The sides had been left unstitched to just below the level of the ribs—both to accommodate the bulky bandages and to make changing their drains and tubes easier.

I peeled the cotton nightdress upwards and, for a brief second, saw the swell of a woman's breast. Then it disappeared under the white folds of cloth. I felt my chest tighten, made myself go on with the examination. I began cutting through the thick wad of bandages, but my eyes were dragged again and again to the sight of the girl's pubes: a

43

reddish fuzz glowed high between her thighs, as if she'd been shaved for the surgery, and the curly hairs were beginning to grow back.

Iodine, I told myself, swabbing the area with an alcohol dampened cotton ball, all the while I felt Ruth's eyes watching me. I began carefully going over the hip and abdomen area, tossing the used cotton balls into a tray Ruth held. I was looking for any signs of puffiness or infection around the long snaking incision, the angry-looking crosshatch of the sutures, but my heart was thudding at the sight of the dark V between Abby's pale legs.

I swallowed uneasily, but told myself I had to know. Ruth was standing just alongside me, and I bent over the girl, putting my back squarely in the older woman's line of vision. I lifted the neat folds of the nightgown, made my voice as casual as I could. "We just want to make sure there's no edema up along your side, Abby."

Her eyes fluttered, she took a deep breath. I saw the firm round of her right breast, a nipple as thick and brown as a cough lozenge and, just beyond the swell, a patch of long red tendrils of hair under her arm. With my left hand, I kept the sheet covering her; with my right, I probed her underarm, as if I were palpating the lymph nodes.

My fingers touched the silky hair, and I was suddenly, shockingly fully erect. I withdrew my hand so quickly it grazed the swell of her breast. I felt my lips part—heard the sound of a soft moan—but it was Abby.

"Did I hurt you?" My throat was tight.

Her eyes opened at the sound of my voice, she shook her head, no. "It itches—"

"Healing," I coughed into my hand, trying to get control. "All wounds itch when they're healing."

"No," she pointed, waving her finger in a slow sweep across her lower abdomen.

"Here?" I asked gently pressing a spot just south of her navel.

"No, lower." Her right hand lighted on the small thin rubber tube of the catheter.

"Perhaps it's loose," I said, my mind turning to medical details; if it were dribbling, the uric acid would make her uncomfortable.

I bent closer. My fingers closed on the flexible rubber, I was aware of the warmth of her skin, I smelled the lingering scent of the alcohol, and I tried to re-insert the narrow red catheter gently—there was a faint smell of violets, as if she'd bathed in a warm tub. I pressed the tube upward…..Violets. Regina…Regina….

Her hips switched rapidly, and my fingers slid lower so that the pads touched the damp glistening vulva, the folds falling over my knuckles.

I jerked my hand away, the catheter suddenly popped out, and a small warm spray of urine spurted out. Abby groaned softly. Even with her eyes closed, her face looked narrower. It had the clean lines of an older woman's with none of the smudginess of youth we call puppy fat—

"She's wet herself. I'll clean it," I heard Ruth say. "There, there, it's all right." She moved forward, her hand smoothing the girl's cheek.

"The tubing's tricky," I said, lying. "Especially on young girls—they're so—" The words died in the paste of saliva in my mouth. Abby (was it Abby?) was looking at me with a sharp intelligence, her eyes sparkling with a dreadful mirth. My heart was thudding in my chest. Abby's lower lip was caught between her teeth, and I knew, I knew she'd come. It could not be Abby, no. I felt myself blanch, fought to control my voice. "I'll send Doctor Saunders in to check Ellie," I said, turning to the older woman.

"All right," Ruth said, nodding.

When I looked back, Abby seemed to have fallen asleep, and her face was round again, her skin had taken on the clear translucence of childhood. The smell of violets was gone.

I stared at the small brass circlet of the housekeeping keys at Ruth's waist, they jingled softly while she moved around Abby and the noise sent wave after wave of vertigo through me. I left quickly, shaking.

Gabriel Wickstrom had told me if I wanted a drink I should hunt him up. I wanted one quite badly—certainly more than I'd ever wanted one in my drinking days at school.

6

"It's the clothes," Ellie giggled. "Her clothes. It makes it easier for her to come through."

Abby nodded. She plucked at the frill of cotton lace disappearing in a froth under the quilt.

The twins were in the nursery, lying side by side and propped on their canopied bed. Now of course, they were no longer one, no longer joined. It was a week after the surgery, they were still bedridden, and Ruth had dressed them—once again—in clean nightgowns that had been worn by Regina.

"Not just worn—*owned*," Abby said, and I wondered if she read my mind.

"Can you tell us apart," Ellie added, and they both began to laugh.

"I only looked in to say goodnight," I said, still standing in the doorway, one hand resting on the jamb. I was aware that my palm was wet, the painted wood a little slick where I touched it. I took my hand away, folded my arms. I would not go in.

"Scaredy cat," Ellie said. Her eyes, even in the fireglow, were very bright.

I swallowed nervously. I'd avoided doctoring either of them since that day, but now in the semi-dark of the room, the image of Abby's churning hips floated on the edges of my brain, the sound of her cries were ringing in my ears. Not Abby, I told myself, Regina, Regina, Regina!

It was Saunders who rescued me. I heard his step, then a second later he was at my side.

"Go to sleep now," he told the girls, leaning inside the room. "Big day tomorrow, we're going to get you up and walking. I want you to get your rest."

The lamp was already out. He shut their door abruptly, and I felt relief wash over me as I moved down the hallway toward my own bed.

"I can't, I can't, it hurts!"

Tears streamed down Ellie's cheeks. Her small hands were firmly clasped inside her father's blocky palms. He was trying to lead her step by step across the nursery. Abby had just made the same trip successfully. I'd noticed her balance was slightly off, but then, she'd spent 12 years walking in tandem with her sister. She was seated now on the low hassock, her legs straight, her bare feet peeping out from under the hem of Regina's old nightdress.

"Do it, Ellie," she urged her sister.

Ellie closed her eyes, shook her head. Her face was a study in misery. Her left leg was drawn inwards, the foot lagging behind her right heel.

"I think she's more frightened than anything," I said to Saunders.

"No," she wailed, "it hurts." She dropped one hand, rubbing it gingerly alongside her flank, and with the motion, she swayed, her knees buckled and she was one faltering step away from collapsing onto the floor.

Saunders leaped forward and caught her.

Ellie shrieked, and this time, her left knee did give way. Saunders managed to get his arms under her slight body, and he laid her gently on the bed.

In an instant, he had her nightgown lifted and he was examining her. I took a step toward the bed, but hung back, half afraid to look at the child's body.

"Perhaps it's just a temporary weakness in the adductors," I said, closing my eyes, reciting from memory. "I've seen scissor gait treated with leg braces, passive exercises—then when she's strong enough and the muscles have been built up, she can move to a series of active—"

"Are you really that dense?" Saunders turned, hissing at me. "Look at this—"

I took a step nearer, and followed the line of his gaze. It was what the old timers called "hot flesh." Ellie had an infection brewing underneath the incision. The skin had gone red, there was swelling. There was no suppuration yet, no smell, no yellowish dribble of pus where Saunders gently pressed the girl's hip. We'd caught it in the early stages. "Wound gangrene," I began—

"It's osteomyelitis, you jackass," he snapped at me. "An infection in her bone."

"I know what it is," I said.

Saunders gave a snort. "Then you know what we have to do," he said.

"Surgery," I nodded uneasily, because I also knew what the treatment of choice was for clearing up infections in bone and bone marrow, and it wasn't something Abby or Ellie should even guess at. My eyes met Saunders's grey ones, and I knew he'd read my unease.

"I'm going to try and inject gentian violet first, and mercurochrome," he said softly.

The gaudy colors of both solutions—brilliant purple and sunset red—swirled in my mind. Both worked sometimes, I knew, but it was that other treatment, the one Ellie would wake to, that made me faintly queasy.

"No more operations," Ellie said. "Please." I saw she was not only frightened, but her eyes were dilated with fever as well. "I'm afraid by myself," she whispered.

"I'll stay with you," Abby soothed. "I'll be there when you wake up—"

"No!" Saunders and I shouted at the same time.

Both girls' eyes had gone round, they knew something was amiss, but they didn't know what. We did.

"Let's get her prepped." Saunders's voice was dead, dry.

I nodded, not wanting to picture what would come next: The treatment of choice for bone infections was simple and chilling. You inserted maggots deep inside the dark red marrow…and you let them eat.

7

If it had been high summer I suppose we might have kept the secret from the girls. Gabriel or myself could've scouted the nearby fields for a rotting woodchuck or raided the local butcher's garbage tin for guts and offal. But it was mid-February, and although every ten years or so there'll be a wild extravaganza of nearly hot, sunny days before winter returns, it was still cold, with a thin snow-cover crusting the lawns and roadsides.

I don't know how she found out; but every day saw Abby more mobile, so perhaps she read the text of the Western Union Saunders sent to the Medical Supply House in New York City asking for meat maggots. Or maybe she was watching when Gabriel left empty-handed for the train station and returned with the large brown-wrapped package, his nose wrinkling at the thin smell coming up from inside the layers of paper and glass.

Or maybe she was peering through the keyhole when Saunders barked orders at me to hurry and I clawed at the layers of paper insulation to expose the large bell-shaped bottle. Inside was a huge greenish lump of rotting flesh shot through with holes like aged cheese. Winding and burrowing through the narrow tunnels—covering it in places like clots of moving string—were the pale bloodless maggots.

I know my stomach heaved at the sight. And it was a thousand times worse when I uncorked the wide mouth of the jar and placed the foul meat on a white enamel tray, then watched as Saunders picked the worms up one by one with a forceps and inserted them deep in the bony pocket where Ellie's hip and thigh joined.

I watched them dive, wriggling, beneath her soft skin that was a bruise of nacreous flesh and mottled trails of gentian violet, mercurochrome; and even if I knew that now we were fighting to save her life, that whether she walked without a limp was not the issue, I looked at the squirming mass and the gorge rose in my throat.

Perhaps Abby heard the sound of my running feet when I dashed for the sink, or the thick ragged noises I made when I bent, vomiting, over and over and over again.

In any case Abby knew, and she told her sister.

"Please. You've got to take them out." Ellie's eyes—normally china blue—had gone the dark of a starless night with fear. "I can feel them gnawing at me," she whispered. "I close my eyes and I hear it...." She swallowed, and now I saw thin tears spilling over the crest of her cheek.

"Do you want to lose your leg?" Andrew said. "If that infection spreads, it means an amputation."

"I don't care, I don't care," she moaned. "I'm not dead, I'm not dead, yet!" Her neck muscles strained, she tried to sit up. Andrew eased her back down, no one spoke for a moment. Then Ellie said softly: "Every time I shut my eyes I hear that hideous song, 'The worms crawl in, the worms crawl out, in your nostrils and out your mouth....'" Her voice, high and sweet, suddenly trailed off.

I stared at her, her face tight and hollow with terror, her small freckled hands clenching and unclenching the hem of the white sheet, and I thought, *it's not a healing, it's torture. We're going to drive this poor child mad*—

"It's so dark in my head," Ellie said. "Just as if I were dead."

Andrew went to his medical cabinet. I watched him upend a vial of sodium veronal, plunge the needle inside the stopper and draw the liquid down into the glass syrette. "This will make you sleep, Ellie." He went to her side, took her arm lightly.

She pulled away. "I don't want to sleep. Take them out or let me die," she wailed.

"Hold her," he said to me.

Then he pushed the sleeve of her nightgown up, quickly swabbed the skin. I saw the needle sink into the thin flesh of her arm, and she cried out briefly.

A few seconds later, she was asleep.

"I'll stay with her a while," Saunders said, rubbing his brow. "You go," he paused. "Go and talk to Abby, find out what she said to her sister. She—" He stopped, his gray eyes met mine. "She won't tell me—she won't even look at me," he finished.

He sat heavily in a narrow straight chair next to his daughter's bed, his face tight with anxiety.

I was nearly at the door when I heard him ask softly, "Stuart, do you think we can still save her leg?"

I shook my head. "I don't know."

"The cut," he said, his eyes going far away. "We would have to cut so high up." He rolled the bridge of his nose between his thumb and index finger. "It will be worse for her than if I'd never attempted the separation. She'll never walk. She might die. Oh, Ellie," he said, and his eyes went to her sleeping form, the soft rise and fall of her narrow chest. "Ellie. Never. I never meant it to be like this." Then he sank forward, lowering his face into both hands, and behind the veil of his palms and fingers, I heard him weep.

There was nothing I could say to ease him; I knew that. I left the office, the sound of his soft crying—as haunting as the ceaseless rush of a dark millrace—in my head.

8

The nursery was empty, the room itself heavily shadowed between the dark velveteen drapes and the waning light outside. I'd expected to find Abby reading or playing quietly and now I stood on the threshold, briefly puzzled.

Where was she?

I peered, squinting, into the dim recesses; at the same time I heard a low humming. It came from everywhere and nowhere all at once. It was like the sound I imagined the old sailors described when they spoke of singing sands.

Aaaahhhhhaaahhhh—

It was thin, rising and falling, a thready tune that drew one along its length, now dipping now falling—

Aaahhhhhahahhhh—

There was such a beach I'd read about in Massachusetts in an old whaling village on Cape Ann. I thought of ships wrecked on jagged rocks, of siren songs and the smell of salt....

I strained, listening. The humming grew louder, and now in and around the vibrating note I heard soft music. I smelled brine—the sharp tang of sweat and body fluids.

I felt mesmerized, and I blinked to clear my mind, my head pivoting in a slow circle. I opened my eyes, and now in the semi-dark of the room, I saw a woman seated before the banked fire, brushing her long auburn hair, the sound a crackling whisper as she stroked and stroked. She was humming the strains of some ancient ballad. I smelled salt. And violets.

She broke off suddenly and turned to me, smiling. She stood up, and I saw she was a tall woman. I guessed the crown of her head would fit neatly just below the cup of my chin.

I felt my heart skip a beat. There was nothing—nothing at all—of Abby in Regina Cahill.

"Where's Abby?" I asked, stupidly.

"Did you ever hear the expression, 'Be what you want to become,' Mr. Granville?" She paused while I shook my head, stunned by what I was seeing but could not really believe. "No? Well it's more popularly known among actors, I suppose, than medical students." She laughed lightly. I saw the red tip of her tongue protrude; she was wearing a set of small rice-sized freshwater pearls, and then, very delicately, she plucked the loop from her throat and absently put the necklace between her teeth to lightly suck and bite on. I felt my heart speed in my chest, then caught the drift of her words.

"...I suppose there are moments when even a student sees himself as a full-fledged surgeon, but actors—those who live—truly come to life—on the stage, they become what they must be. Have you heard, Mr. Granville, of those who live the parts they play, who eat and drink and fuck inside those minds?"

I was startled, and I flinched. This was 1893 and it was the first time I'd ever heard a woman say that word, and if you must know, to this day, even in this place where I am confined, where I've routinely seen women handle themselves—plunge their own fingers up the bloody tunnels of their raw and aching vaginas, I've never heard any woman say it out loud.

She went on. "Yes, to emotionally understand the part, those actors simply *be* what they must become. So even the simplest action...walking, or say, eating a meal in character—handling two dessert spoons primly or gaily tossing popcorn from the striped pasteboard box to their flung back mouths—becomes an exercise in being." There was a faraway look in the green eyes as if she were seeing deep into some other life. "But whether I have become Abby or she has become me, I don't know...."

"Ah. Abby," I said, and I heard the quiver in my own voice.

Regina fastened on that note, and I felt in that minute I was somehow hers.

"You love her," she said.

It was true. I knew it was wrong, had sweated night times that I was twenty and she was barely twelve; at the same time I'd played a thousand fantasy games while my hands caressed myself: Abby was a respectable nineteen, and I was twenty-seven, and after she took my garnet ring beneath a fat yellow July moon, I made love to her in the deep shadows of lawn and hedge—the greens nearly black, the grass damp beneath our churning bodies.

I listened to those words from Regina and I wanted to sob: I did, I did, I loved her.

I'd told myself a hundred times that it was absurd; that I only felt I loved the child because I was trapped in this madhouse with no companionship, nowhere to go, nothing at all to ease my foolish undergraduate heart. I chided myself that I was aroused only because my sympathies were being played on. Here was a poor crippled girl...who became whole when my hands touched, healed her—

"I—" I stopped. What was there to say? For every voice that shamed me, cried it was lunacy, there was another part of me seeing her heart-shaped face and brilliant blue eyes looking seriously into mine the first night and telling me to have compassion for her poor father—he was not himself because he drank. There are cripplings of all kinds. And I knew without trying or meaning to, Abby had touched the part of me that understood the silky sinister thought she could not say out loud: and if he's tied to his obsession, then so am I.

"What you don't understand Mr. Granville," Regina said, "is that there are no hauntings without the consent of the human who participates."

"Yes, I do, Mrs. Saunders," I answered, feeling a certain steel rising inside myself. "You're going to trot out that old chestnut—if a tree falls in the forest but no one hears it, does it make a sound?" I snorted in protest, but she cut me off.

"But it's true—do you think I'd be here without their fantasies? Their fantasies of being with you—and more to the point—of being me—of being a grown woman with whole limbs?" Her hand went to the white liquid of the silk gown she wore, and she began rubbing the column of her thigh. "If most girls want to be their mothers, then how do you think crippled girls melted inside their own bodies feel, hmmm?"

I knew she was seducing me, and yet, I could not help being drawn in. Perhaps if Abby had been older—an eligible perfectly normal young lady of eighteen who had a crush on her school master—I might have turned on my heel and left that room to pack my bag and never have given her a moment's thought. Not even if her crush permitted her to send me sentimental puppy dogs cards at the holiday season, or vacation scenes with deserted beaches from the Jersey shore. But Abby was, by virtue of her great infirmity, a child with a woman's mind, and I loved her mind.

Regina's huge shiny olive eyes bored into me. I don't know which of us unlaced the slippery tie that held her gown closed I only knew that she was in my arms, and that it was Abby I held, the child grown tall. And although I let myself be lost in the moment, and shut out the part of me that knew precisely what I was about when Regina fingered the buttons of my fly and begged for the whole hard length of me, and though the higher, better part of my mind knew that taking her was sad and wrong...in truth in my heart it was Abby I loved, and Abby I made love to.

9

I woke sometime later under a drift of quilts and counterpanes that cozied up the girls' bed in the nursery. The room had gone very dark; the only light was the low reddish glow from the fireplace on the opposite wall.

The bed was warm, and only half-aware, I snuggled into the heat, burrowing into the featherbed and under the covers. Part of my mind searched for the webby outline of some delightful dream I'd just emerged from.

Then suddenly and all at once, I remembered what had happened and I sat bolt upright, my heart pounding in my chest hard enough so that I heard the pulsebeat thudding in my ears.

I could see the humped and scattered shapes of my clothes lying pell-mell on the carpet, but I was alone. I threw my head back, snuffling the air for the scent of Parma violets. All that came back to me was the doggy odor of sweat and sperm. I imagined the stains that would lightly green the nursery sheets; Ruth did the laundry, what would she think? Then I was aware not only of the bed's warmth, but of a heavier dampness. In my mind's eye I saw my jaw pressed greedily between Regina's full thighs.

I pushed the covers back quickly. Running my palm lightly across the spread of white fabric, it seemed to me there were dark blotches and smears among the wet.

I lit a candle, found my suspicions immediately confirmed, stifled the groan rising in my throat. Blood. It was blood, and I wondered if was a full-grown woman's menstrual flow or the hymeneal blood of a virgin child.

10

I was dressing when I heard the unmistakable sound of a child sobbing. It was not loud, but it was the kind of terrible weeping that went heart deep; ragged, hitching, the breath coming out in violent broken gasps. It seemed nearby. Feeling my face flush hotly, I went to the cherry armoire that stood in the corner and jerked the door wide. Nothing. Ranks of clothes, gossamer slips. A row of black leather high-topped shoes on the floor, all neatly buttoned.

Then I recalled there was an attic room just overhead on the third floor. Seldom used, it was known simply as Regina's closet. I snatched the short fat nub of an old candle stuck in a wax-clotted saucer from the dresser. Then, shrugging my arms into my jacket, I left the room, crossed the hallway, and began to climb the stairs.

Abby was sitting in the small white gabled room, her knees drawn high, her head bent under the tent of her arms, her hair hanging down like a nun's veil. She raised her face at the sound of my footsteps, and I saw her eyes were hideously glazed with confusion and pain. The skin of her cheeks and lips and chin looked raw and abraded, and unconsciously my hand went to my own jaw and I felt the burn of stubble. No, I told myself, that red chapped skin was because she'd been crying; my eyes went to the small eyebrow window. It was closed, but the attic room was unheated, chilly.

LISA MANNETTI

"I thought you cared, but you hurt me," she whispered. I set the candle on the bare floorboards, and stared at her. "I wanted you to kiss me, but what you did—that thing—it tore me—" she stopped, and my heart jagged sharply in my chest. A child, you took a child. Raped her. *No. It was Regina—a woman's heavy scent, full breasts, birth-widened hips—*

"I hate you," she hissed.

"Abby," I said, stooping close to her. I wanted to touch her shoulder or her hand, but I was afraid. "I saw your mother—"

"My mother." Her voice was bitter, her small mouth twisted into a harsh line. "My mother is dead!" She screamed, her face was contorted, she lunged at me. I held her elbows, felt the tiny hard knots of her fist striking my thighs. I held on, lifted her up. Her hands pummeled my chest over and over.

"Ssssh, sshh, now Ab, Abby," I crooned mindlessly, feeling the fury pulsing out of her. I let her pound her pain into my flesh.

"She lied—she lied to me, to Ellie—to us!" Abby wept.

"Lied how, darling?" I asked. She was quieter against me now, I stroked the soft fall of her hair, felt her cheek in the hollow beneath my rib. "How did she lie?" Abby made a muttering sound, something I could not quite comprehend, I tilted her shoulder away so that her face was turned to mine. "Say again."

"I didn't know what it was." She blushed, and I knew if she'd had the nerve, her eyes would have fallen on the full space in the fork of my crotch; but she was too ashamed and fearful. "I didn't know what men had, what it was between men and women," her voice was the hiss of a writhing snake.

Not anger—but terror and shame, I told myself. I heard her tiny helpless voice in my head: I wanted your *kisses*, Stuart. It jibed badly with the joking obscene voice I'd heard begging and felt breathing hotly against the soft smoothness of my ear, a husky woman's plea:

Fuckme, Ochristfuckme.

64

A kind of peculiar understanding knifed through my brain, and I turned the child's chin up, made her eyes meet mine.

"Abby, do you remember that night in the nursery when you and Ellie told me the story of your mother's death?"

"No." She shook her head, holding back tears; bravely, I thought. Her reddish curls swished softly against the thin shoulders of her bleached muslin nightdress. "Didn't you tell us stories? That woman, Scheherezade—how she saved her own life beguiling the sultan?"

In my mind's eye I saw them, Ellie and Abby, like twin dolls gazing blankly at the ceiling, their faces immobile, their arms lying woodenly at their sides. Who, what was there, listening, and sometimes talking to me? I raked my hand through my hair; Regina's green eyes, sharper features rose in my mind. No. It couldn't be! I tried again.

"You told Ellie we had to put the maggots inside her hip to clean out the infection...."

"Ellie...maggots?" Abby's face was blank—as if what I was saying made no sense. There was no connection between writhing white worms and her sister's condition in Abby's mind.

I was getting panicky. "You *told* her," I insisted more loudly. "Now she's hysterical!"

"It wasn't *me*!" Abby's face turned with a sudden dreadful quickness towards the night sky-blackened window. I saw her small freckled brow, the mane of her reddish hair and the white knobs of her shoulders reflected like fragmented ghosts in the dark panes of glass. She cried out and, heaving herself, I felt her jerk her body, trying to leap and run towards the window. I caught her, held on tightly.

"No, no," I said. My mind was a whirl. Had Regina possessed the child? Had Abby's mind been broken somehow? Or is it you, Stuart? A voice mocked inside me. Did you rape a child and tell yourself you gave a grown woman what she wanted? One of us was mad—one, I mourned—or maybe all.

"Let me, let me die," she cried. Her skin scalded my chest.

I had heard of possession, of demons, of the dead reaching out to snatch at the souls and bodies of the living. Is that what it was? Impossible. Such things were the stuff of inmates' dreams.

There is no such thing as haunting without the consent of the human who participates.

"I feel so dirty, I didn't know anything could feel so dirty. I want to die. If I die it can't hurt—not like this, not this much."

"No," I rocked her gently, waiting for calm to take her. "Have you seen Regina?" I asked Abby.

"Something." She touched the center of her chest with a small dimpled fist. "In here. Not seen, but felt and heard. In the wind at night, in the small voice that whispers in my dreams. I hear her call my name. But she says her own name until she and I and Ellie are the same. No division. A strange and peculiar joining, odder than the freakish twist of nature me and my twin shared."

She said those words—things no child could ever say, and again I felt my mind twirl. Who spoke that pain? Woman? Girl?

God, it was madness. I felt my own tears, hot and hard. If there was even a chance that Regina Cahill Saunders was real, had come back, if there was a chance she was some organized intelligence, then I knew she held us both in her thrall.

I led Abby away from the window. "Here, carry the candle," I said. She snuffled for an answer, and though she picked it up, she was still lightly crying. She sniffed, scraped the sleeve of her cotton nightdress under her nose, and the gesture was both so child-like and unselfconscious it went straight to my heart, as children's innocent movements often will.

I hugged her—a father leading his child to safety— round the shoulders as we slowly descended the narrow wooden stairs. She held the candle aloft, her eyes following the careful track of her bare, blue-veined feet. At the bottom of the stairs we shut the thick attic door, and turned toward the nursery. Abby wept, and I did, too.

But whether I cried for her confusion or my own, I did not know.

11

"**S**tuart! Stuart!"

I heard my name bellowed in my ear, and I woke groggy and tense all at the same time. I'd been dreaming that Regina Cahill was walking down a blue walled corridor, a mauve silk dress swishing around those infernal hips. Her smiling rosy mouth was a bud. "It's not over, Stuart," she was saying. A frilled parasol popped wide with an audible sound over the glossy auburn curls. Her green eyes, meeting mine, were saucy. "No, it's not over till I say it's over. And it's not over."

I was attracted—oh what a lie! I could feel myself throbbing while we sauntered; and casually, I folded my palms behind my back. *All the better for you to see my hard-on my dear*, the slavering big bad wolf spoke up in my dreaming mind.

"Stuart!"

Now the dream fell away in shreds and tatters and I was sitting up awake, aware that whoever was calling my name *was* real. I heard that shrill cry again. It was Saunders, he was at the bottom of the staircase and he was screaming for me. I knew at once he was desperate and the fear that was coloring his voice was because Ellie was in mortal danger. I did not even bother to check whether I was dressed or naked. I sprang from the bed, bolted from the room.

My shirt was flapping round my bare thighs as I sprinted for the hallway, but the chill I felt as gooseflesh came from his words:

"Ellie! Ellie! We have to do it now! Now! Her fever is 104! If we don't try and take it now, she's going to die."

Before I was slamming my bony heel onto the third step I saw the surgery clearly in my mind: The first cut—the dark line of maroon blood like melting red pearls—transsecting just beneath the iliac curve, the silver clamps like metal butterflies sipping at the juncture of the femoral artery. Ten minutes and it would be done. Irreversible. Over. I saw the careful black sutures, stitching through fascia, tendon, muscle, flesh. The hideous flap of free-hanging skin from buttocks and thigh folded up to cover the gaping hole. In a few days there would be swelling at the wound sight. The wound we inflicted. We would have to drain the swell of her stump.

Ah Christ.
We were going to amputate her leg.
Take it.
Her leg. Ellie.
But it was that or her life.

"Please," he begged, "close it." Saunders coughed deeply, his hand palmed the center of his chest, and although I knew these days had taken a toll on him, what I saw more clearly was that his grey eyes had the desperate burned out look of a man who understood only one thing: there was pain, and that pain could be lost in the bottom of a glass. There were drugs in his closet that would carry out the same chemical command faster and quicker, and we were living in a time when drugs that can't be got now for love or money...heroin, morphine, cocaine...were available, and yet he wanted his alcohol. It was the craving for the smooth liquid brown of brandy I saw on his face, as clearly etched as if he'd said the word. He flapped his hand, the hem of his always proper black frock coat faintly echoed the motion, and he sailed out the door. I heard the cellar door open with a sloppy scraping sound—he wasn't drunk—not yet. But his mind was disordered; his movements, jerky.

"Gabriel," he bellowed. I heard the smash of glass. In my mind's eye I saw ancient green bottles pulled from their diamond-shaped slots in haste, exploding on the hard cement of the cellar floor.

"Gabriel! Christ, come and help me!"

There was broken weeping coming from a distance, but I knew the hired man would answer the summons, uncork the bottle; and though his mental state would essentially be in no way different, now Andrew Saunders would drink. And drink. 'Til the fevered part of his mind let him sleep.

I turned to the job he'd asked me to finish. In essence we were done. Ellie's leg—the whole god-sculpted lovely length of it—from just below her hip was gone. Before he'd decided there was no more a doctor—a father could stand—Andrew had wrapped it in a sheet and placed it on the bed her sister had lain in when we'd done the initial surgery. My eye snagged on the sight of it, a long tubular hump hidden under the drift of white. Dead. Useless. I looked away, concentrated on my work.

I stitched; small neat silken sutures. I did it as carefully as I could because I was blocking the fact from my mind that there would be no prosthesis for Ellie. No wooden leg that could make up the deficit. Andrew was right. The cut was too high.

Beneath my focused, careful fingers I sensed/heard the faintly wet thrip and felt both the tiny poke of the needle, and, as I twisted my wrist, the corresponding minute catch in the living flesh. Ellie was alive. Her father and I had saved her. And her twin might dance and twirl and run in meadows when the autumn grass was waist high, wheat brown. But never....

I glanced down at the oval cross section of her thigh, so like a dark, oozy depression in the rotted hollow of some ancient stricken tree. I was tucking the ugly envelope of skin around her wide stump, closing the wound...but never, I thought. She would never walk.

12

It was a week later; Ellie was drifting in and out of consciousness because Andrew and I were keeping her dosed to the eyeballs on painkillers. I do not think at that point she even knew her leg was gone. But, for a moment, if you will, imagine waking to that knowledge. Remember, if you can, the dreams—both simple and complex—you sheltered in your heart as a child. Did you see yourself magically made pretty? Think you'd be taken into the neighborhood club? Or suddenly liked where you'd been scorned? Getting even? Becoming rich? Famous? The dreams of days of promise. Remembering those moments, imagine being a freak for the brief twelve years you slept in your bed, ate breakfasts, fought with your brothers and sisters, breathed.

Ellie had been afraid of having the surgery, but I know a part of her dreamed of being set free—so imagine her reaction when she woke—and found herself worse off. Yes, worse off. Because when she was tied to Abby she had Abby— a sister exactly like her self. She had another living human being who shared her life and her pain. But now she was a cripple—crippled and alone.

It was nearly midnight, when I looked in on my patient. Ruth was sitting nearby nursing Ellie; alongside the older woman's knee there was a knitting bag disgorging the woolly bulge of a partly completed sweater, and on the doctor's narrow wooden sofa table, a thick black bound Bible.

"She's asleep," Ruth whispered, answering my unspoken question when she heard my footsteps outside the office door. "Poor thing, she doesn't know what she'll wake to."

I nodded somberly, watched Ruth get up to dampen Ellie's brow; she was wringing the sponge, the water tinkled softly in the basin.

"We saved her, though," I said coming into the room, my eyes adjusting to the dim yellow glow of the shaded kerosene lamp. I found myself idling over the open page of Ruth's book.

"Yes, I know that, Stuart." She pointed with her thick chin toward the Bible. "But I just can't seem to get it straight in my heart. Don't understand at all why the Lord would make a child suffer so. An innocent child."

"Yes," I said. I lit a cigarette. There wasn't any rhyme or reason to what had happened.

"I know all about what those Orientals believe, karma and such. And I tried to get my mind around it," she said, softly moving the brown puff of the sponge over the girl's cheeks. "But there's no sense to it. None. Don't care about past lives and all that truck. Even if that stuff's true as dirt, nobody deserves to come round again having to cope with more than Jesus himself up on the cross."

"And did you find the answer here?" I asked, tapping the thin onion skin of the page with my index finger.

"Nope. Maybe I didn't really expect to. My heart was just so full, and I thought to ease it with something I'd grown up with—old words are comforting at times. Or maybe I'm just trying to do what I always done—take care of Ellie and Abby so as to make up for my own past."

She averted her eyes, I wanted to ask her what she meant, but found I didn't have the nerve. I toyed with the thin pages of the book, not wanting to look at her or Ellie.

"Regina never cared a damn for anyone—she only thought of herself, you know," Ruth said. "After she killed herself, I tried to understand that, too." Her closed fist tapped the center of her bony chest just over the place where her heart lay. "But I couldn't. I'm plain enough—the young men of Poughkeepsie used to joke that my body was all right, but my face could stop the court house clock. But Regina...she was so beautiful...physically beautiful." She sighed, then went on. "Like I told you, I'm not an educated woman. I'm not even a smart woman, but I went out and I bought a copy of that there Frenchman's book, *Emma Bovine*—"

"*Bovary*," I corrected automatically.

Ruth nodded and in the low light, I saw the yellow flare of the kerosene lamp reflecting in her spectacles. Her voice was sad, I thought. "I heard tell on it at the Vassar College library, and I thought that was maybe like her—driven, living with a man she didn't want, so frustrated she'd destroy her own life to get what she thought she needed."

"It's a brilliant book," I said evenly.

"Yes and it's just as real as real. But that kind of knowing—it's just like the Bible, Stuart," she indicated the heavy black bound book. "It changes nothing."

"Ruth," I began, but she cut me off.

"Regina's here in the house!" Her hand went up as if she were taking oath in a courtroom. "I've looked in at the twins many a night, gone in to make tucks and kiss their foreheads, and I've smelled that bitch Regina's fancy violet bathsalts and seen her face leering out of one of theirs—"

"Ruth!"

"It's the solemn truth. And something else," she said, drawing a deep breath that made her rib cage rise. "There's been times when I've heard the rustle of her dress, or her laugh floating down the stairs—that evil sniggering laugh!

75

God knows I know her voice well enough and that laughter's a living thing that can move around corners or travel on a straight course same as the smell of baking bread rising out of the oven."

Her face had gone dark, her mouth was knit in a tight line, and I knew she never expected me to believe these things. She saw me as a man of science and I think part of her hoped, wished I'd say anything—no matter how harsh or insulting—and pull her away from the thrall of her fancies.

"I've seen her too," I said. But before I could say more, Ellie was beginning to stir uneasily.

"She's coming round," I said. Her eyelids were fluttering, her face, which had been slack and expressionless was beginning to show the discomfort of pain at a low level awareness.

Some part of Ellie seemed to know. And the first thing we saw was her hand dabbling and making passes over the vacant spot that began just below her groin; then from six inches away, her half-sleeping hand traced the carved out space moving up toward her hip—where she had been joined with Abby.

"Unnnnnhhhhh" a deep groan escaped her.

She began to cough and hack so fiercely my mind jumped immediately to hypostatic pneumonia. She'd been lying on her back too long. I was afraid her lungs had filled with fluid. She coughed again. Her left hand dove toward her groin and her eyes flew open.

"My leg, my leg," she cried out. Her small cat face was a mask of terror. Ruth's big hand was digging in Ellie's shoulder, and over and over she was mindlessly crooning, soothing, "Sssh, sssh, there now, there now, get a grip, child."

"My leg!" She burst into a terrible spate of weeping that made her cough harder and gasp for breath. Her red hair clung to her forehead in sweaty strings. She could not stop crying, and I believe the truth of the matter was so awful, she could not, would not, did not want to accept it. She tried to sit up. Her hand was clutched against the heavy wad of dressing, the dead end of what had been the very top of her thigh—and more. "No," she screamed. "No! No! Not my *whole* leg!"

Ruth tried to hold her back, but Ellie catapulted forward sitting up and instantly all three sets of our eyes were riveted on the thick, heavy dressing rising vertically in place of where her leg had been.

"I want my mother," she shouted. "I hate you—I hate you! And I want my mother!"

"Ellie!" Ruth's eyes went wide, her voice was a strangled plea. "No—don't say it! Take it back, take it back quick!"

"Mother!" Ellie screamed again.

Not three seconds went by that I did not see a dead calm steal into Ellie's eyes and then, Regina's hard, crueler features moving over the child's face. Her hair went the darker shade of mahogany. Her form filled out; there were breasts pushing up the broad white hem of the sheet.

My eyes went wide, and I'm certain I gasped, called out, "Ruth, Ruth do you see that?" My own breathing filled the well of my ears with an alien sound. I don't know what she said in reply. My gaze was fixed.

Because most unbelievably of all, beneath the thin film of the bleached cotton sheet, a long shapely woman's leg—a true phantom limb—filled out the sad void that was the missing space of Ellie's stump.

"Get out, Ruth," Regina hissed through bared teeth, a clenched jaw. "Get out, now." Her voice had a thick timbre, it rumbled deep in her throat, the hideous bubbling sound of someone speaking through a clot of mucous—as if she had to learn to use Ellie's voice box. But Regina's dark jade eyes were very bright with malice.

I watched her swing her legs sideways. I felt my heart starting in my chest. Regina's bare feet flapped against the floor. Then she began to move woodenly away from the bed, as if she were not quite used to manipulating this surgically impaired body, this child's form. Her arms were held out stiffly, her legs gave way to a lurching gait.

Ruth wasn't fooled. "Where's Ellie now, Regina?" she said. Her voice was as stern and uncompromising as I'd ever heard it.

Regina's laugh was hollow. "Inside me. Thrilling to the movement."

"Let her go," Ruth said. "She's just a child!"

"*My* child. And therefore mine to do with, just as I please."

"No one owns anyone else, Regina."

"I owned you, Ruth. Didn't I?" Her eyes narrowed, her mouth narrowed to a red slash—a terrifying imitation of a smile. "Why don't you tell Stuart about it, hmmm?" She flung out one hand limply.

Ruth winced. Her face went the color of old brick. She cringed, her shoulders turning in on themselves. "No," she gave out a soft gasp.

"No, you won't tell—or no, you don't believe I owned you?" Regina was very calm now—as if she might begin doing nothing more important than filing her nails or sipping tea. "'A plain woman, whose body was all right but the young men of Poughkeepsie said my face could stop the court house clock,'" she mocked. "Oh yes," Regina went on. "Ellie might have been unconscious, but *I* heard every word you said."

Ruth shook her head, her hands clenched into fists at her sides.

"*Tell* him, Ruth," Regina brayed, throwing her head back. "Tell him where I found you and what you were doing!" She turned to me. "And to think you were worried about her finding stains on the nursery sheets," she tssked. "Ruth knows all about such stains, don't you?"

"That's enough, Regina!" the older woman shouted. "Shut your filthy mouth!"

"I daresay your mouth is just as dirty—dirtier, in fact." Her eyes went the harsh green of glittering emeralds. "Know where I found her? In the county jail. Know why dear, Bible-reading Ruth was there? Because she was running a young Christian girl's Sunday School. Only the real agenda wasn't studying what Jesus and Mary did. The real learning took place in Ruth's bed! A cot in the alcove behind the curtain. Young men, indeed! It was girls *you* liked the taste of, wasn't it, Ruthie? Gabriel didn't know. He was my hired man, and he married her—then he found out though, didn't he? Didn't his pals tell him, 'Gabe you've married the female whore of Red Hook.' Maybe that's why you never had children of your own—Gabriel certainly liked fucking me!"

Ruth ran at her. I was too slow off the mark to prevent it. She raised her heavy arms, and it was then I saw she held the glowing kerosene lamp. A groan spiraled out of me, and I leapt forward.

But not before she'd hurled the light at Regina's head.

I never knew if at the last moment some semi-sentient part deep inside herself caused Ruth to change her aim, or whether Regina thwarted it. I saw Regina blink, she stepped aside, and the kerosene lamp whizzed past her striking the large mirror on the opposite wall. The glass exploded outward with a huge crackling noise. Glittering shards danced madly in the air. Then, as if the fiery orange reflection itself held power, the flames and glass streamed back toward Ruth as quick as the furious trail of a burning comet.

Ruth began to shriek. The top of her head was alight, and in the instant she put her hands to her hair, they caught fire, too. She screamed again.

I snatched at the bedcovers, wrenching myself so hard I felt my back muscles twist in an agonizing spasm. The thought flashed through my mind that I'd been standing scant inches away from Ruth, that I *should* be burning, too. But I threw the covers over her head and shoulders, trying to smother the flames. Ruth was coughing and sobbing at the same time.

"Got you now, got you now," I called, holding onto her swaying figure and trying to half carry, half drag her to the rumpled bed across the dark smoky room. *Oh dear Christ,* I mourned, inwardly. The smell of charred flesh, hair, wool was thick in the air. Ruth coughed. The wracking sound and her moans were muffled under the heavy pad of the blankets.

I heard the noisy scuffle of running feet from the second floor, the slam of the cellar door, someone shouting indistinct words. But underneath those sounds and the chaotic whirl of my own madly chattering brain, I heard another: the dark glee of Regina's low laughter.

The door to the office was jerked wide. Andrew and Gabriel crowded the threshold. "What happened, what happened?" the hired man shouted.

In the glare of the lamp he held high and the sting of my own watering eyes, I saw what he and Andrew found:

The dark room with its wisps and threads of eddying smoke; Ruth wheezing, sprawled on the bed, her head and face swollen with lump-like blisters, her hands flailing in the drifts and clots of burnt-up hair. And Ellie out of her sick bed and lying right cheek down on the cold floor, her good leg buckled nearly beneath her, the wound of the stump leaking blood and pus.

13

"**I** ought to send you out of my house this minute, Granville," Andrew said.

It was a half hour after he and Gabriel had stormed into the office. Ruth lay anesthetized between us on the table.

I didn't answer. I knew whatever I said would only make him angrier. But in his voice I heard his belief that if I'd watched Ellie more closely she'd never have lost her leg, that she would not have been lying on the floor. Worse, I heard his accusation that it was somehow my fault that Ruth had been so grievously injured.

He passed a trembling hand over his wet brow. I saw his drink-bleared eyes go out of focus and his attempt to bring himself back to mental alertness. His gaze sharpened, but I knew he'd come to the stage where he didn't trust himself or his own judgment; no matter how incompetent he thought I was, I was sober.

"I ought to hang up my shingle, turning Ruth Wickstrom over to a hack like you...."

I looked down over the rim of my cotton mask; her normally expressive face was hidden under the mucky swamp of the burns. Her nose was putty melting toward her slab of a chin. There were only narrow blackened remnants of her lips; I knew that whatever reconstructive surgery I could manage there would be nothing more than two rubious lines of scarified flesh—nothing to what human lips were at all.

"All right," he glared at me. "Just do it."

I nodded at Andrew Saunders, and I picked up the enucleator—never letting myself think about what a cold term, what a nasty instrument it was—then inserted it like a pry lever. A moment later, the white, fishy heat-boiled globe that had been Ruth's brown right eye was cupped between my gloved fingers.

14

A week later Ruth was conscious. It was twilight; the room was gray with shadows when I went to her sickbed in Saunders's office to check on her. Her brown mummy claw of a hand snatched at my white medical coat as I bent over her.

"You got to get 'em out Stuart, or go yourself." She stared hard up at me.

"You hearing this?" she asked. Her voice was more hiss than whisper, the result of her burnt lungs. Her lips had trouble making the words.

"Yes," I said. "But how?" I let Ruth's hand dawdle in the folds of fabric coating my chest.

"Send 'em to school—somewhere," she stopped to catch her breath. "Abby's smart. And they'll take Ellie, even if she's a cripple, to get Abby on board. There's not many places'll scruple at double tuition. You send 'em on to one of them schools in the city, or if old Andrew balks at that, one of the girls' seminaries in Connecticut or Massach—" she paused, and I heard her breath whistling in her throat.

"There now—easy," I soothed.

"You're a fool, Stuart Granville." It wasn't quite a yell; she couldn't manage that. But her good eye bored into me. "Don't you know now they're separated Regina can take 'em when she will? Don't you know as a spirit she's bound to the place? But she'll get stronger, and if she does, sure as Satan, she'll burrow down inside their minds. What then, Stuart. What then, henh?" She coughed, but she was too weak even to stifle it with her fist. I touched my hand to her mouth tenderly.

"Andrew will never let them go—he'll say he hasn't got the money, and he'll resent me for interfering," I said. I stroked the cropped wiry mat of her hair.

"I'll tell you what then," she went on as if I hadn't spoken. "Regina will win. She'll get so strong that whether they're here inside the house or not, it'll be the same to her." She licked her lips. She didn't ask, but I poured from the pitcher and handed her the glass. She sucked the wax-coated paper straw briefly. "Thanks," she muttered. "You're a good nurse." We both smiled at that. Ruth's smile was the light in her good eye—her lips were too raw to stretch into something we all take for granted.

"I turned it over and over in my mind a thousand times. What else have I got to do—lying the livelong day in a bed? I think maybe Regina could only come through because the girls were separated. A body can't be in two places—two minds at the same time. And even a spirit might be bound by the same law."

I held the glass so she could sip at the straw and drink again.

"Don't wait, Stuart. If she gets too strong....I believe it was her plan all along, a way to get—not just out of the grave—but out abroad into the world. Think of it, the girls going out into public for the first time, why, if she gets enough of a hold on em, she'd sail right out the front door with which ever one was carrying her at the moment." Ruth closed her lids. Looking at the right one was like seeing a paper shade sucked half way through a broken window by a draught of wind: The wrinkled flesh sank, partly, into the empty space.

"Ruth, Ruth," I said, lightly squeezing the sensitive hand I took in mine, "but I'm nothing more than a hired man." I dropped her fingers, raked my hair. "Same as you and

Gabriel. Do you think Saunders will listen to me? All he has to do is utter the word 'expense,' and I haven't a defense left in the world. How can I tell a man what he can afford or not?"

She didn't answer, but her face took on a hard look. I saw her hand clench at her side into a tight fist as if she'd instantly made up her mind to say something she didn't really want to—not at all.

"You know good as me *why* they should go away to school."

She knows about Abby, I thought, feeling my jaw muscles knot.

"I always thought I'd be here to look after my girls." She swallowed hard, and I saw what was left of the corded tendons in her throat tense. "Even if I loved Abby and Ellie—and I did—I had to learn to love them in a different way." She would not look at me, not even so much as to let her good eye wash over my chin. "It was a lesson. They were my penance." She turned her head, gazed blankly at the far wall. "Now, they're yours."

I felt her hand groping for mine.

"Lord, Lord," she whispered and squeezed my knuckles white.

15

I only saw Regina twice that long summer. And I believe now, Ruth—even during the time she was bedridden—held her back in some way. Or perhaps she was subdued by my sudden mood swing away from lust toward innocence. However it was, that summer—with its days of heat and blossoming and freedom—was in so many ways Abby's first. I saw her pleasure in simple things—catching fireflies, stretching her hand to snatch the highest fat blooming pink rose from the wooden arbor, inveigling me to play statue tag by moonlight—and they brought a delicious tropic heat that stole the agonizing winter from my heart.

"It's hot—even for night," I said. It was August, we were on the porch, a gibbous moon skimmed the treetops.

"I can do a cartwheel," Abby announced. She let go of the crank on the ice cream pail she'd been turning. Her face was flushed with exercise; in the glow from the house lamps I saw the beads of perspiration glimmering on her upper lip. She skipped off the porch, batting absently at a mossy hanging pot filled with wilting petunias.

"You're supposed to be making ice cream," I said, pointing at the 'freezer.'

"Strawberry." Her pink tongue skated across the line of her lips. "Yum."

"And wasn't it your idea to have an ice cream supper?"

89

She'd read about them in the newspaper, boys and girls sitting at the long trestle tables under the trees at the Methodist Church or in Deer Gate meadow. Wanted to have one—with lemonade, and the best tablecloth, all of us dressed up—sitting in the yard. I couldn't make her understand it was called a 'supper,' but it was really a kind of social where desserts were served; you were supposed to eat something—some kind of dinner at home—first. It was hot, none of us wanted to cook, and ice cream for supper seized her mind. I'd given in, of course.

"You crank, it's nearly solid and hard to turn," Abby said.

I nodded, adding more sugar, dumping in more of the plump red fruit.

"You're not watching my star turn," she said, putting her hands against the crisp, summer stunned grass and churning her legs over her shoulders. Her dress—white muslin with a blue satin sash—belled upside down over her torso. There was a twinkle of pantalettes, the white toes of her stockings. I turned away to crank the ice cream freezer.

"Pantalettes are hot," she said, now sitting cross-legged in the grass. "Can I take off my stockings?" She didn't wait for my answer, but began tugging at the sweat damp silk.

"You're spoiling that child," Ruth whispered at me from the shadows. She was sitting deep inside the cushions of a heavy wicker chair. Gabriel had carried her outside. She was stick thin, a folding tripod of a woman beneath her wraps.

Before I could answer, we heard the faint squeak of wheels: Ellie's chair moving over the threshold, out onto the porch boards. Like her sister, she was wearing white, too.

"Help me, Stuart," Abby called, skittering up the steps. "I want to get Ellie onto the lawn." She began to maneuver the handles on the back of Ellie's chair. I steered and lifted it down the broad shallow stairs, while Abby yapped and ran around me like a puppy.

She began pushing her sister in circles on the dry grass. "It's almost ready," she announced heading for a circular moonlit table set with big clear goblets, folded napkins, spoons; then: "Is it ready yet, Stuart?"

"Nearly."

"Ice cream. Cartwheels. Best white dresses," Ruth shook her head. "Even you—in a linen suit."

"She's had so little—I don't consider this an indulgence at all," I said, waving my hand over the freezer. The girls were having a race now; Ellie pumping the chair wheels hard, Abby hopping on one foot to make it fair.

"That child is in love with you," Ruth said. Her face was swathed in a veil of white gauze. I saw it sway lightly from the puff of air when she spoke.

I'm looking at a ghost, I thought.

"What's the age of consent in the South, Stuart?" Ruth said. I heard one sharp creak of the rockers, the soft pat of her toes.

"Twelve or thirteen, maybe." My lips tightened in a narrow line, I kept my eyes on the hand turning the ice cream freezer. I wouldn't look at her. "I don't really know, it wasn't—isn't—a thing my family held with."

"Ever had a girlfriend?" she asked.

I gasped. "Ruth, please—" I begged.

I heard the rocker moving against the boards again. I saw her hands lifting the crown of her veil—as though she meant to remind me of her dreadful staring face. "People with nothing are relentless," she said. "Answer me."

"It's why I drank." I swallowed uneasily. "Why I started drinking and kept on with it. The first Christmas I came home from college we were both seventeen. We got engaged. It was fine between us all that month. Then I got back to school—it wasn't other girls—there weren't any in my class. Well one," I laughed. "But she had a mustache and could lift a hundred pound sack of grain one-handed over her head." I felt Ruth's eyes on me, pushing me deeper inside the old memory. "Livvy—Olivia, that is, who was my fiancée, wrote me every day. You know, the kind of gushing letters...." I suddenly sat on the porch rail, staring at my hands. "Letters about how it was all going to be when we got married. Even," I breathed, "even what kind of furniture we'd have. Our babies she said—they'd have her thick blonde hair and my blue grey eyes."

"Yes," Ruth said. "It's just the kind of thing a girl spins out in her mind. Scared the hell out of you, I bet." The rocker snapped forward.

"I felt like there was a chain around my throat." I laced my fingers together. "The more she wrote, the worse it got, the worse I felt. At the end there—just before I wrote her— she was sending sometimes two letters a day. All that love and good will and sweetness—it pulled on me. The nicer she was the more obligated I felt, and I didn't want to write her more than once a week maybe, or have her write so much. But she did." I paused, drawing my cigarettes from the flap of my white linen jacket. "I didn't answer for a long time. The mail was like a drift of white in my letterbox. My roommate used to joke me about it. 'Must be a relief to see a bill from Klegg's Department Store or The Blue Angel Cafe,' he'd laugh handing me the pile."

"Finally you wrote and told her," Ruth prompted.

"I didn't want to be engaged anymore—didn't think I wanted to get married. Not when I finished medical school, maybe not ever." I lit the cigarette; the air was so still it stayed in a thick cloud around my head, and the thought crossed my mind, that Ruth and I were alike: our faces shrouded by the mix of shadow and white.

"How'd she do it," Ruth said.

"Livvy—she jumped from the Tide Basin bridge. Drowned."

"Was your letter in her pocket?"

I nodded, sucking in the smoke, feeling half-drowned, myself. "Everyone knew," I whispered. The flush of guilt and shame washed over me all over again. There's no more terrible feeling in the world, really.

"You drank to kill the guilt," Ruth said. "And I guess, like Andrew, you found out pretty quick it doesn't work."

Abby's high laughter bounced toward us from the garden. I heard the thin scratch of gravel: the wheel chair on the paths, her footsteps. We could hear the girls moving toward us.

Ruth leaned forward now, quickening her speech, lowering her soft voice even more. I had to strain to hear her. "Did you know that when Regina was pregnant with the girls, she had bad trouble with her heart—the beats, too fast."

"Palpitations," I said.

"Just so. Andrew gave her some kind of drug—not once, but every day to slow it—"

"Barbiturates," I guessed.

"When the girls were born like they were, they blamed each other. This house was hell a long, long time."

"Of course it's ready," Abby's voice came to us from the side yard. She stopped pushing her sister's chair briefly, and we could hear her take a long deep breath. "Phew, hard work, I think you've gotten fatter, Ellie," she laughed.

"You want to watch out Stuart," Ruth whispered. "Your guilt helps conjure Regina. Needing her to take the sting out of being with a child."

"No more, Ruth," I warned. They were maybe forty feet away—the length of the porch. I could see the white shapes of their dresses just beyond the shrubbery.

"She loves you, too." Ruth ignored me, bearing down on the *too*.

"Regina?" my voice was a strangled caw.

"Ellie," she answered. "Don't let the same lesson get by you again." She tugged my sleeve, forcing me to look at the matte of veiling. "Some people—the ones that are weak and too wounded—they aren't strong enough to live with love that's not returned."

Abby bounded up the steps. "Let's just eat it right here." She waved a set of spoons she'd snatched from the table. "Right out of the freezer, Stuart."

I went to get Ellie, heard Ruth telling Abby to hold on and wait for her sister. "Go call your father, Ab," Ruth said.

Andrew staggered drunkenly onto the porch, moving haphazardly through the long shadows; he was collarless, in his shirt sleeves.

There was a metallic thump.

We all jumped at the noise.

"Shit spells," he cried. The ice cream freezer clunked and rattled, rolling onto its side under his feet. He skidded unsteadily in a puddle of water.

I heard Abby's sharp intake of breath.

"It's just ice cream," he announced soddenly. "For Christ's sake, shut up."

I thought he might kick at the freezer, but he turned and went back inside, weaving away from us, the wooden screen door banging shut.

I moved quickly in the silence, righting the can, moving it out of the wet, rapidly turning the crank handle a few times, saying nonsense things like, "It's okay, we'll have it now, it's done for sure."

Then, we were in a small cluster—me and the girls— Ellie leaning over the edge of the chair. "Readysetgo," Abby said, the enthusiasm gone from her voice.

Three long handled spoons dove into the round tin, salty water sloshed at the edge.

"The pail leaked, the pail leaked when he kicked it," Abby wailed.

Ellie's spoon fell from her hand at the taste, a red stain bloomed, ran from her dress front to her lap. She began to cry. "Aren't we ever going to have good times like other girls?"

Salt bitter; I spat over the side of the porch, trying to clear the taste from my own mouth, thinking it was no worse than the taste of Ruth's words.

"Ruined," Abby mourned, "every time I plan something, it ends up ruined." She hurled the spoon, it clattered across the porch.

"Plans are like that sometimes, honey," Ruth said.

Abby ran to me, her head burrowing against my chest. I knew she wanted no more than a moment's comfort. I held her close.

I watched Ruth reach out to dab Ellie's soiled dress gently with a handkerchief. She folded the cloth in a pad and touched the clean part to Ellie's cheeks, blotting tears.

Ellie's sad eyes followed me. I read in them the thought that she loved me but it didn't matter, saw the knowledge she was not chosen, never would be.

I couldn't look at her. I soothed Abby, shushed her, knowing Ellie was aware the tears silvering my own eyes, stinging my throat were all for the summer night gone sour and her twin.

Shortly after that, Regina came among us.

16

"**I** could send you to New York, Ruth. There's good surgeons there," I said. It was just past lunch and we were sitting side by side in the library; on the low table in front of us was a half empty coffee pot, the crusts from two sandwiches, an open surgical text. The photographs were obscure and cloudy, but the illustrations were crystal clear.

"Will the New York specialists fix me up so that people will look me face on?" She stared at me, and I caught the wet glimmer of her good eye under her veil.

"No," I shook my head. "But they can contour the shape of your jaw...." There was no real cosmetic skin repair in those days; we just grafted what we could from healthy tissue to cover injuries and wounds. "Give you areas of scar-free flesh...."

"So, instead of looking like the rusty broken-through bottom of a blackened skillet—"

"Ruth!" She was right, but it didn't stop my shock.

"I'll be like something the tinker left too long on the fire and then tried to mend. Lots of copper-red seams and lumps."

"They have more experience with this kind of thing than Andrew—"

One of her hands had contracted, and she laid its shrunken monkey foot shape on my arm. "I don't want Andrew to do it—I want you to." She paused. "You say the infection's not healing the way it ought, that taking good skin," she touched her left buttock briefly, "will stop the endless oozing and weeping and dressings with picric acid." Her lips stretched in a grimace I knew was a grin. "Stuart," she leaned in confidentially patting my knee, "you can't make me look any worse."

She was wrong of course; and we both knew it. But I thought it brave of her to say so.

It was while Ruth was under the anesthesia—the first time for skin graft, the second to remove the mortified flesh from the failed surgery—that Regina appeared.

It was seven o'clock in the morning, and I'd just excised the first of the long rectangular strips I planned to use to cover Ruth's seared face and throat with healthy tissue. Andrew was working with me—I understood she wanted me to do the surgery—but I needed assistance.

"I keep hearing the word flay banging away inside my head," he said, looking at me over the brim of his mask. His hands were unsteady, he looked hungover, but I thought he was sober.

"Yes, it's like that," I sighed looking at the bloody furrow I'd just carved in Ruth's buttocks. I lifted the skin strip with the point of my surgical knife, and Andrew laid it onto a shallow metal tray filled with saline solution. I started cutting the next section, my mind focused on the details of the delicate operation; Andrew hissed, and I looked up, squinting into the comparative shadows of the room. Regina stood just inside the threshold, the door flapping wide behind her.

"Here! What are you doing!" Andrew shouted.

I'd stopped, the scalpel hung in mid-air, a rill of unchecked blood welled up in the pit of the wound then spilled over the white slope of Ruth's left hip.

Was he seeing her? Shouting at me?

"Doing here," I echoed in a strangled voice.

"Taking care of unfinished business—same as you," Regina said.

I felt my heart clench in a painful spasm, the blood ringing in my ears.

"By the way, Andrew doesn't see me. I won't let him—not yet, anyway," she said. She moved towards the table, hands gripping the padded edge, peering down. "He's only reminded of me—a fleeting thought, a psychic whiff of....violets...."

She trailed off, but I thought she might be about to say which one of the girls she was manipulating.

"Ruth," she tsked under her breath. "Such an ugly state to be in." Her index finger rode the ruined mound of flesh, and she sucked at the reddened tip.

"Stuart, she's bleeding!" Andrew shrieked at me.

I started working fast, but my fingers were slipping in the gore. *Nerve, keep your nerve,* I shouted at myself inwardly, forcing the hemostat against the spurting vein. Acrid yellow sweat dripped from my temples, stung my eyes.

"Clamp it, Andrew! Clamp it, I can't see!" I turned away from the table, quickly mopping my brow with a sterile swab.

"How much did you drink last night?" she asked, coming close and sniffing the air around me. "Your eyes are bloodshot. You're not more than a binge away from becoming Andrew," she said, grinning up at me.

"I won't let you destroy me," I hissed under my breath.

"I won't have to," she said. "It's inside you, you'll do it to yourself." She laughed lightly, then turned shimmying toward the hallway, beige high heeled boots clicking on the bare floor, a tuft of frilled petticoat bubbling from the olive line of her hem like white froth foaming on the sea. She turned, and

I was suddenly aware of her pale arms, the swell of her breasts at the wide neckline.

I shut her out of my mind, went back to the table; Andrew had already staunched the bleeding and turned my patient over. The red swamp of Ruth's face lay under my shaking hands. I was trying to force myself to concentrate, to think.

"Ruth can hear me. Deep inside herself," Regina whispered from the doorway.

I glanced up.

"She's crying with it," Regina made a fist and struck her chest. "But her tears aren't enough." Regina shook her head. "She was a worm using my shame against me to burrow inside my daughters, to usurp my place, make them her own. What if I did hate the sight of them? Freaks squeezed from my body. 'Poor Regina,' they said. 'Look what she gave birth to.' Ask yourself how many mothers can look on monsters with love? Oh but Ruth loved them, did she? She is suffering, and I will make her suffer more." Her smile was a shark's grin. "I will see her dead, Doctor."

Was it Abby or Ellie? I peered harder looking for a clue—the now-familiar habit Abby had of pushing her hair back from her damp forehead with the inside of her wrist; a slight sway in the walk, the psychic residue of Ellie's amputated limb.

But she was already gone, the door vibrating in her wake, shutting her from my sight—but not my thudding heart.

Andrew had prepared the graft site, and we laid the first strip, fat-side down along the length of Ruth's sunken cheek and jaw. My hands still trembling, my mind seething, I stitched as neatly as I could.

It was long and messy and, with a sinking heart I knew— less than half way through—it was a botched, miserable job.

17

September first, a week after her surgery, the large black mortified patches on Ruth's cheeks, forehead and throat told the tale. The newly grafted skin was dying, it had to come off.

"Now what?" she asked, lying groggily against the pillows. The faint odor of decay overlaid with bactericide clung to her.

"Debridement—"

"Meaning—"

"Meaning, I have to scrape the rotting tissue, or there'll be an infection and it will kill you."

"No anesthesia," she said wearily, her good eye hunting mine.

"No," I said, getting up to pace the length of her bedside. "No. The pain—it's impossible." I paused looking at her directly. "It wouldn't be surgery, Ruth, it would be torture—"

"Listen to me, *Doctor* Granville," she interrupted. "Every time she comes out, Regina gets stronger. We both know I can't hold her back if I'm unconscious. You shoot me full of morphine, or whatever drug will deaden the pain, and then you give me a local—or whatever you call it, and you operate."

"Very few people can stand being awake and cut with the scalpel in such a personal delicate area," I said quietly. "It's the intimacy, our faces are us."

"And what is my face now?"

I couldn't answer that.

"Regina can't have it all, Stuart," she said. "She can't keep winning. You shilly-shallied around and look, here it is September, and I'd hoped the girls would be off somewhere at school." Her voice trailed away.

"I was taking care of you," I put in.

She made a snorting noise. "You're like the Dutchboy runnin' here and there plugging endless holes in the dam." She held up two bandaged fingers, lightly stabbing them in a random pattern. "But let's not forget it was Regina who sprung those leaks. Give me what you can to take away the pain—but no general anesthesia," she said.

18

It was only in 1886—seven years before—The British and Colonial Druggist had come out with an article hailing the use of cocaine injected as a local anesthetic as revolutionary. Andrew kept up with things like that. There was a subsequent article in one of the journals, *Lancet*, I believe, demonstrating the technique. Two tiny raised wheals were made, and you advanced the needle while injecting fluid beneath the skin; you stopped pushing the point deeper when you got to the place where you made a slight indentation with your finger against the flesh. Then, still injecting the cocaine, you slowly withdrew the needle. It looked straightforward, it was supposed to be painless.

But I'd never done it.

"Ready now?" Ruth asked.

I'd been in the library the last two hours poring over Andrew's articles and textbooks. Despite what I'd read, I didn't feel confident about the surgery. Regina took that from me, too, I mourned inwardly. Andrew was closeted in his bedroom drinking. We were in his office-turned-surgery, the tray laden with instruments. An apothecary in Poughkeepsie kept the cocaine solution on hand and, while I was familiarizing myself with the procedure, Gabriel had brought me the white paper-wrapped package.

"Sure," I said, taking her hand briefly. "Just keep that brown charmer of an eye closed, and we'll both come through fine."

Ruth squeezed my fingers for an answer.

"Well, then go ahead," she said, and I saw her hardswallow a lump in her throat. "Poor Gabriel. Much as he took on, I don't believe he bargained for this."

"There, there now," I soothed, at the same time I watched the colorless liquid squirt up from the syringe when I cleared it of air bubbles. I winked at Ruth, then I made the first injection.

She gasped a little, wincing at the penetration of the needle, but when I stopped and stared at her, she waved me off as if to say, *Pshaw, it's nothing keep going.*

I allowed time for the cocaine to numb her, and few minutes later I began to cut.

The first half hour, I'd swear that between the morphine and the subcutaneous injections of cocaine she felt nothing. She was doing her job of lying still and I was doing mine of cutting away the failed graft tissue.

But the infection had run deep and maybe it was in the moment I forgot she was live and awake under my fingers, and I incised more deeply.

"Ahhhn," Ruth groaned.

"Okay?" I asked from behind the gauze mask and looked down at her.

"Keep going," she whispered, and I felt her hand squeeze my wrist.

Certainly, I should have noticed that she was flinching, biting the inside of her lips. Instead I was conscious of the juncture of old and new skin, of grayish areas teeming with

104

spent cells. I thought I saw signs of what we call necrotic—a fancy word that means dead—tissue. I should have given her more morphine, injected her again. I held the scalpel blade at a flat angle, slicing close to the bone.

Ruth gave out another short sharp cry.

When I looked at her again—looked at her as a total patient—it was too late. Stoic that she was, she'd finally passed out from the pain, and Regina was in the room.

"You've certainly made her look far worse than anything I ever did," Regina said, peering over the table. The air was hot and heavy, she was plying a lavender and black lace fan.

"No, there's a difference. You hurt her. I'm trying to heal that damage."

"The way you healed Ellie?" she taunted. "Ellie's certainly better off one-legged and confined to a wheelchair."

I saw the fan fluttering just below the level of those mocking jade eyes. Tendrils of the auburn hair swirled around her face. Without thinking, I seized her wrist, squeezing hard. "Bitch. You want to play games?"

The fan clattered to the floor between us.

"Which one are you, which poor child have you tucked inside your rotten heart this time?"

She laughed and, instead of resisting my grip, she nuzzled her chest against mine, ground her hips against the arch of my pelvis.

"You're not a real woman," I said, shaking her off and pushing her away. She stumbled slightly, then caught her balance. She stood facing me, her face bright with malice.

"Maybe," she said. "But I'm the only one you'll ever have—unless you count Abby and Ellie," she giggled.

"I can have my bags packed in half an hour and be a hundred miles from here before sunset."

"Try it," she said, leveling her gaze at me.

Something in the way she stared made me think of those times last winter I'd tried to break away, about the feeling I had of being tethered to the house by some invisible cord. Something that drew me back—almost against my will. True, I'd run a few small town errands while Ruth was down, but even then I was uneasy. The house loomed large in my mind. I would hurry back, telling myself I needed to check on her, on the girls. More and more I'd fallen on the hired woman's habit of having what we needed delivered to the door—

"Even shoes for the girls," Regina whispered. "Imagine what Mr. Cramer and his fat frizzy wife think when a letter comes to their store with a foot traced on it, saying, `I'm not certain of the size but please send two pairs of good black high button shoes and two pairs of white kid to fit.'"

I felt my face go red; I thought of my scrawled notes to the library, the candy shop, the hatmaker...it never occurred to me how strange it must look.

"Even stranger if the Cramers knew one shoe of each pair was wrapped neatly in paper and stored in a trunk. Why don't you tell them to send a pair and a half, hmmm?"

"Go away," I said, suddenly tired, scrouging my fists against my eyes. "I have work to do." I turned my back on her and returned to the operating table. Ruth stirred when I injected the cocaine in the raw wounds, but she was still unconscious. I worked on removing the infected flesh, told myself I would finish what I'd begun—

"So will I," Regina said, giving voice to my thought.

When I looked up some forty five minutes later, she was no longer in the office. But overhead, from the nursery, I heard the muted tones of a low song.

I stayed by Ruth's bedside all that night, watching over her. At first, I thought she was drifting in and out of consciousness; she moved, spoke—muttering through the cocoon case of bandages swaddling her head. It was only later on I realized something else—some otherworldly intelligence—was using the dead space of her mind to communicate with me.

"Regina has a plan," she whispered. Her hand, lightly resting in the cradle of mine, twitched. I squeezed gently.

"I'm here, Ruth, I'm listening. Jesus, I was afraid I'd lost you." I felt a clot of fear and sorrow rising in my throat, my voice hitched a little, and I paused. "How's the pain?"

"I been seeing visions and things a while now," she said, not answering my question. She was lying on her back, one hand a limpid starfish spread just over her heart. "Since the burning." The white balloon shape of her head churned slowly against the pillows as if she were straining to see the landscape inside her mind. "It's cost me some strength, holding Regina back; but I wanted to give the girls their chance, wanted to give you time to heal."

"Me?"

"You been hurting a long time—these scars, this burnt up, half-blind face—they're just Regina's way of showing you your own heart and mind, Stuart. And I'm afraid," she said softly. "Afraid it'll get a lot worse before she's done...with all of us. She wants to kill Andrew," Ruth began.

I leaned closer to hear: her voice had taken on a strange muffled quality. It wasn't the weight of the bandages; she sounded as if she were speaking from the other side of a heavy pane of glass. I felt a low vibrating tone that gave me the shivers.

"But first she wants your child in her belly."

"How is that possible?"

"I don't know," Ruth said, and her head swiveled and shook against the pillows. "Some things are not given for me to see. But I hear the word "false" hissed over and over in my mind, moving like writhing vipers in a pit." Ruth passed a shaky hand over her good eye, its light winked out behind the white scrim of bandage. "Regina is playing out an old drama...as if...as if you were John Price the young tutor whose baby she carried and Andrew cut from her. This time she means to bring the child to term. I see her in an empty garret room—like a fat spider weaving dreams and plots. She sits rocking, singing to herself, waiting. That waiting has been her hell—and she means to escape it."

Visions of Regina—full-blown and pattering through the house—rose in my mind. I thought of the night I heard her story, of the girls mewling *Only one can be chosen, only one can live.*

"Does she mean to divide the twinship, to pit Abby and Ellie against each other?"

"She has done it already." Ruth said, and her voice was a low sigh, the lonely sound of wind in ancient pines. "It will be up to you to bring them together—and suffer the consequences." She opened her good eye, her look—filled with dread and sorrow—pierced me. "I don't envy you, Stuart. I'm only going to my death—your path will be much harder."

"Don't I have a choice?"

"There is always choice; but what looks like salvation is often just a darker web." She paused, gathering her thoughts and went on. "You got to keep a lid on your fears and suspicions, Stuart—if you don't you'll be caught in her trap— and the only way out will be your own destruction."

"Ruth," I begged. "Help me. Tell me what else you see." But she had gone inside herself again, and there was no rousing her.

19

"The Missus won't stay another minute," Gabriel said, his head hanging, his fingers clenching the brim of his felt hat. He kept his eyes fixed on the shabby colors of the carpet in the library, shuffled his feet. "I just come to say good-bye, Stuart."

I nodded. Six months had gone by since Ruth's original 'accident,' six weeks since I'd tried to repair the damage. There was no overt sign of infection, but she was growing weaker. She would end what was left of her days still wearing the heavy veil, venturing out at nightfall in the deepest shadows. I knew she wasn't leaving because of the vile mass of tissue scarring, but because she was afraid if she died in the house, Regina would be able to dominate the girls completely.

"There's things she says she's got to make up for yet" He stopped.

"Where'll you go?" I asked.

"Does it matter?"

"To me, yes, it does."

He sighed. "I've a brother up New Hampshire way; he's a kind of farmer. Oh the house ain't much more than a shack compared to the elegant monstrosities up and down millionaire's mile here." He waved one arm in the direction of Route 9 and the huge mansions and fields where Roosevelts played and Vanderbilts sported. "We don't want elegance, now. Just a certain solitude. No one knows Ruth up there—don't know a thing about her. Probably won't, 'cause she'll stay close to home, and my sister-in-law, Claire'll look after her."

"Will you write, sometimes?"

He smiled at that. "I s'pose you and the girls can look for a card come Christmastimes."

We shook hands. From the window I watched him striding toward the curtained carriage parked in the dooryard. I knew Ruth's bundled up figure was already inside. A thickly gloved hand showed briefly, parting the drapes, softly turning in a short farewell.

"Ruth," I whispered.

Then Gabriel snapped the whip, the horse trotted forward, and they were gone.

It was Autumn now; the library was darkly quiet, the ticking of the clock too loud. The sound of the coal furnace exhaling heat through the pipes rattled me.

I got up and paced, briefly. Now there were only four of us locked in with the demon; a third of my protection gone, I mourned. Regina had been quiet lately, biding her time I thought, while Ruth recuperated from the last of those miserable surgeries.

I'd only seen her a few times since that day. Once she came to supper in Abby's place and Andrew never noticed a thing. Another dusk toward the end of September, I glimpsed her evil features leering at me from the wheelchair Ellie had been slumping in just a minute before. When I looked again, there was only the misty lawn shimmering in the twilight, the curtains billowing out from the open windows, and she was gone, leaving Ellie's thick lumpish body in place.

Childishly, I wished the Wickstroms had stayed on. It was wrong of me, but I knew that some primitive part of me believed if Regina had Gabriel and Ruth to torment, she might leave me alone.

DISSOLUTION

My answer to these thoughts was the sight of Regina wearing a low cut rose-pink gown entering the library. Her dress swished as she moved through the door. I started, seeing that just below the neckline of her gown—in the place where her breasts jutted outwards—someone had drawn red inky circles over her nipples. She was smiling broadly. More ominously still, I thought, she carried a pair of long silver scissors, the light glinting malignantly on the metal shears.

20

"A thought is a summons, Stuart," she said. "And, I'm so very glad you called me." Laughing, she began to snip through the bodice of her dress. "I'm only showing you what you want, Stuart." The top of the dress fell away, she cupped her breasts, fingers splayed around the heavy nipples.

"Well, you're wrong. Dead wrong." I looked away.

"It's the dark whispering part of your mind, Stuart. Not what's on the surface. See?" She hissed. "There's no red circles of ink drawn on the dress." She turned the flaps of cloth upwards.

My glance snagged on the shiny satin. There was nothing there.

"Undercurrents, Stuart. The things you don't even let yourself *think*. You wanted to see my breasts, caress them. Believe it." She began to squirm out of the gown, pushing it down towards her pubes. The soft scritch of the satin was maddening.

I swallowed uneasily; certain when I looked again, she would be nude. Which of the girls was it? I wondered. Which one had let her in?

"Which one do you want, Stuart?" Regina said.

Her mechanical laugh pierced my flesh like hundreds of sharp pins.

113

I hesitated, saying nothing. In that brief waiting, I saw Abby's eyes—large and sorrowful—looking into mine. I saw her small form—the tiny buds of her breasts, the not-quite fleshed thighs. I even saw her left knee and the purple bloom of a bruise where she'd accidentally run into the newel post not two days before. A moan ran out of my throat like water gushing from a pump. She flew into my arms; or maybe I took her up—but she was there, realer than real—and we held each other once more.

I laid her softly against the worn carpet in the library, scarcely aware of the chill rising from the floor.

"Stuart, ah Stuart. Gently, gently now," I heard her whispering plea against the lobe of my ear.

And yes, yes, I wanted to take her sweetly, slowly. If I'd been too rough before, too hurried, I wanted now to initiate her, to bring her to the brink with tenderness. She loved me. I knew it, and I wanted her to find her own depths knowing I loved her and cared, too.

And yet, yet, I found myself ripping at her clothes, pressing a pair of urgent lips against hers, groping with all the finesse of some potentate ravishing a slave from his concubine.

I took her gasps for pleasure, and I took mine, until she cried out and I saw on her thighs, the marks of my greedy fingers.

Then I heard Regina's shrill laugh in my ear. "I like it hard and fast, and I like it more than once," she crooned huskily. I drew away, and for one heart-stopping second, I thought I saw Ellie's round adoring eyes peering into mine. It was more than any man could conjure in a fantasy, like having all three of them at once. If I'd been an artist, I suppose I'd have seen the swaying bodies of Botticelli's three Graces in my mind. Separate and united in their eternal dance. And yes, I'd have sworn, the body bucking in time beneath mine was pushing itself side to side—one hip rising higher—the result of the amputation. But before I could draw back, look down, I heard the library doors pulled wide.

Andrew slammed them immediately. There was no doubt this time he'd seen.

21

"Jesus Christ!" I drove myself to my knees, snatched at the rucked folds of my black wool trousers. My thighs were suddenly cold. I struggled to my feet.

A hand flailed, clutching at my wrist. "Let him go," Regina hissed. "He'll drink himself into a stupor." She shrugged. "If he remembers it at all, he'll think it was some disordered dream: a nightmare and nothing more."

Her eyes were very smoky, like the dull fern-green of a misty swamp on a hot southern day.

"Don't go," she said.

I thought of Abby, Ellie, Regina, merged and writhing beneath me. And I let myself fall inside her embrace.

Regina always had her way with me. I only wish I'd understood it wasn't me she was wanting at that moment. I was merely an inconvenience to be taken care of. She didn't want me to spoil her plans. She didn't want me to interfere. If I'd gone to Andrew right then, we might never have had the argument that led him to go on a sodden two day binge. Regina wanted him pig-drunk.

Drunk, he would be so much easier to kill.

22

"**H**ow many times have you fucked her?" Andrew screamed so loud, spittle flew from between his lips. His face and throat had gone purple with rage. The veins and tendons in his neck stood out like ship's rigging.

I'd finally gotten the nerve up to leave the library and face him. We were in the long upstairs hall; now, seeing his rage, I tried to back away from the confrontation. I kept walking, moving past the silent wooden slabs of the bedroom doors, edging towards the huge bay window. The unused toy sheep was flotsam bobbing against the sea of the carpet strip....

"Come here, Ellie," he barked sharply.

The nursery door opened behind me. I heard the creak of the wheels, stifled a moan thinking how much better we'd all have been if the surgery had never happened, if the whining rattle I heard was the old whir of their toy's wheels.

"I want you to look at her, look her right in the eye. I want you to look at this helpless crippled girl," he said, "and then I want you to tell me how it feels to impregnate a child?"

My eyes brushed over her thick figure, the image of her clinging to me like a barnacle rose in my brain. Once. It was only once, I told myself, and it was more illusion than reality. A kind of fever disordered me, but I saw the swollen waist, the rising breasts hidden in her slouch, her loose dress. Impossible! Not in the half hour that had passed since I left Regina. I shook my head.

"Big man, think you're a *man!*" He moved clumsily towards me, his fists swinging in roundhouse arcs. Broken sobs poured from his heaving chest with the hollow sound of someone beating on an empty steel drum. "You betrayed me," he wept.

He staggered blindly, lurching. His feet suddenly went out from under him, he was deadfalling toward the window.

"Papa!" Ellie shrieked.

The glass shook in its frame, I heard a loud crash like the concussion of fireworks, but I caught him; my own heart was thudding in my chest, my mouth filled with the sharp metallic tang of fear.

There was a spiral of bloody red cracks floating in the glass. The skin of his scalp had given way under the blow.

"It's just a split. I wasn't cut. The glass isn't even broken." He felt his forehead, then wiped the dripping blood from his forehead and cheek. "But, you should have let me fall, Stuart," Andrew said raggedly.

And as he said it, I had the sinking feeling he was right.

23

"**Y**ou want revenge? You'll have it, Andrew! Over and over! Forever!"

I was cowering in my narrow bed: Regina's crackling voice came to me like the sound of rats scratching in the walls. For nearly a day and half, Andrew had been rampaging drunkenly through the house, shouting, smashing furniture.

"The only revenge," his voice went deep with terrible rage, "I want is to send you back into—"

"Hell? I'm going to be your hell! Hahaha!"

I heard the sound of scuffling, heavy tramping feet.

"Break it, break it!" she shrieked.

There was gargling, a rasping choke.

In my mind's eye, I imagined Andrew's fingers pressing the flesh of her slim throat.

"Bitch, bitch," he panted.

"Go ahead. Snap it and send your daughter to her death!" Regina hissed.

"Papa! Papa!" came the plaintive wail.

Andrew began to weep, and I knew she'd suddenly withdrawn leaving the terrified man gazing into Abby's or Ellie's fear-hunted eyes.

A second later, her vicious laugh rang out again, tormenting, confusing him, and he screamed—inarticulate cries—over and over, until he was hoarse.

Then his voice trailed off into a broken whimper. "She's not real. She can't be." I heard him arguing with himself. "Get a grip, man. She's a pink elephant. You have the D.T.'s." I imagined him holding up the spread fingers of a badly quaking hand, watching the waves of the tremor. Instead, I heard the festive pop! of a cork, and I knew he was drinking again.

Later, there was a dreadful quiet, their venom spent. In those moments, I got up from my sour, unmade bed and held my breath. I padded across the room, stood listening at the door, my head hanging, my ear cocked. No sound, nothing.

I could imagine her hand lighting on me when I sneaked down the staircase, her screaming glee. I felt the sweat breaking out hotly under my arms, stinging. I crept into the kitchen for scraps of food.

It was like a siege in some war-torn city, but by dusk of the second night, it seemed Andrew had finally been overcome by drink and his own exhaustion. His bedroom door slammed shut a final time and then, the drawn-out stillness of the house lay like a palpable thing—heavy, brooding, malignant.

Was Regina biding her time? Laying a trap?

I finally found my nerve, and oozed softly down the hallway to look in on the dark nursery.

Both girls slept like felled oaks.

24

I was sure that when Regina murdered Andrew the twins' personalities were entirely submerged, that they were no more than vehicles—empty vessels Regina filled with herself. I'm not so certain anymore. But they say evil is dull and repetitive, so perhaps that's why Regina chose the same means she'd used for her own suicide—a drug. She couldn't force him to eat it, so she injected him.

I imagine her only regret was that drunk as he was, he was unaware and no pain—no death agony—showed in his face.

I found him the next afternoon around five o'clock. He was lying on his side in bed, a small brownish pool of vomitus under his gaping lips. His gray eyes were wide and staring.

I'd spent the day convincing myself he was finally sleeping off the combined effects of his fury and a hangover, although the growing dread I felt in the center of my chest told me I was doing a poor job at self-deception. When I couldn't stand any more of the gnawing silence, I went to his room, tapped hesitantly at the door, opened it.

Even then, in the dim shadows, my first thought was that he was only asleep. The room was close. I smelled the reek of sour wine, the cheesy odor of his stomach contents.

"Andrew," I said, moving toward the bed. I heard a tinkling noise; something I half-trod on snapped, then rolled away.

I saw the cracked hypodermic, the steel needle slightly bent, shining against the wooden floor, and I knew the whole story at once as clearly as if I'd seen it.

I stooped down, pocketed the evidence, my mind flashing on the coroner, the undertaker I would have to call. Then I screamed for Regina to come.

I could hear her soft laughter springing around me, like water bubbling from a hidden well. It seemed to play against the very walls of Andrew's dark room. I turned, expecting to see her tall nimble figure moving through the doorway. But there was nothing—only the thin spray of her laughter, shifting and tossing, higher, softer, louder.

"Regina, Regina!" I shouted; then stopped, suddenly realizing it was useless. She would not come, Andrew was dead. It was up to me to take care of the arrangements, do whatever I could to hide his murder.

He'd been dead for about eight hours, I guessed. I saw his corpse was in the first throes of rigor mortis: His lower jaw and the back of his neck had gone hard. When the flow of circulation had stopped, the force of gravity had drained the blood downward, so his face and throat were waxy pale. I knew that stagnant, pooled blood purpled one ear, the side of his chest, and left buttock. There did not seem to be any visible needle marks in his arms. I checked his scalp, and there was a dot that was probably a mole between two of his middle toes, but nothing more. I couldn't find the spot where Regina injected him, so I hoped the examiner would overlook it, too.

Wincing a little, I unbuttoned his stale shirt. Andrew was known to be a drinker; I put my hands together, fingers pressing downward, gently palpating his liver. It was like massaging hobnailed glass. No one—not even a novice in the medical field—could mistake such grandiose symptoms of cirrhosis.

Still, at the thought of calling in the coroner, I felt a buzzing at the nape of my neck as if my brainstem was an angry, swollen hornet's nest. I would hitch up Saunders's horse, go soon. But first, I thought, rubbing my aching forehead, I had to see the girls.

I should have known Regina had released them: During the day I'd caught glimpses of them through my window playing out in the gardens. Now from the library, I saw Abby strolling on the graveled path, then suddenly chasing a late white butterfly she caught between her hands. She ran to put the delicacy between her sister's. I watched Ellie smile; she held it, felt it tickle her palms. I watched her let it go. It flew around her red head, then lighted once on her shoulder before it took itself off.

The smile disappeared completely as, empty-handed, I approached her and Abby, my feet first crunching over the bluish pebbles, then whispering over the grass. They were both sitting in a small grove of locust trees, the sun slanting through the pale leaves.

"Where's tea?" Ellie demanded. "It's nearly six, and I saw the baker's boy knocking at the back door three hours ago. I want tea and biscuits or cake."

I only shook my head. "I didn't think," I began.

Ellie had gained a lot of weight, some 25 or 30 pounds, I guessed, and her face looked too round, sullen. Her lips seemed to sag under the extra flesh. Her midriff was thick, the bubble of her pregnancy was clearly exposed, but even her fingers had the tallowy look of suet. Some was the result of eating haphazard meals and snacks, of sitting depressed in the wheelchair. Food was one of her pleasures.

"Tell my father we've got to hire a regular woman, someone who'll cook real meals, serve us. I can't do for myself, you know. Abby's no better at cooking—even if she can walk. How are we to live? And what about my baby?"

I stooped down and picked up a blade of grass, not knowing what to say, what to do. I put off the news. Foolishly, I said, "Did anyone ever show you how to make a kind of whistle with grass? You need a long wide piece. You wet it," I said, putting it briefly inside my mouth, "and hold it like this." I cupped the grass blade between the thick humps at the base of my thumbs, blew a short staccato blast. "Try it," I said, handing her a weedy looking dark green snip.

She threw it back in my face. "Who's going to take care of us, Stuart? I heard Ruth telling you to ask my father to send us to school." She began to pant a little with her anger. "She's gone now," Ellie shouted at me, "and I can't go to school and you know that my father drinks. You came here to help us, why don't you help?" Her eyes were rolling slightly; they'd gone the dark blue gray of granite and she fixed them on me.

"Your father's dead." It came out unexpectedly, not the way I'd have chosen to tell the news at all. And certainly, given the training I'd had—scant as it was—nothing like the consoling way one was supposed to take on with families of the deceased. And certainly not twelve-year-old girls. Abby gasped.

"What! What?"

I was still hunkered down, seemingly glued to the spot. "Regina gave him—I don't know—some drug. One or another."

"That's impossible Stuart!" Abby put in. "Ellie and me we've been together every minute."

"He's dead," I said again.

"Besides, Abby said, "after they stopped that horrible argument, we made a pact to fight her off."

Her eyes met mine; I shrugged. The facts contradicted her.

"Maybe she doesn't need us to come through anymore," she said slowly, her voice tinged with bitterness and fear.

"What'll you do, what'll you do," Ellie said, clasping her small hands together. "They'll think *you* did it!"

Something in her voice, something in the way she averted her eyes, or the way she'd been so aggressive when I'd come on them in the garden. Something. I looked at her sharply. Her round, heavy moon of a face was hidden in her hands, but I had a quick mental vision of Ellie suddenly 'coming to' in her father's bedroom, the horror of his death sinking in, the needle dropping from her trembling hands, her body tumbling forward. In my mind's eye I saw her catch herself by snatching at the bedcovers. I heard Regina whispering darkly in her mind, *Mother's here, don't worry, darling. They won't suspect you. They'll think it was him.*

I'm glad he's dead, Ellie had said fiercely. He made me a cripple—he and Stuart.

Calmer now, Ellie dragged her near-dead weight to the wheel chair, its polished wooden seat and caned back glaring at her from the corner of the room where Regina had left it.

I thought about Ruth's warning. Some people can't live with unrequited love. Was this Ellie's way of paying me back? I felt my stomach cramp.

Ellie was conjuring her mother, and whatever pact the girls made, she ignored it.

25

I mpossible. *We've been together every minute.* Abby's word's percolated through my mind, and on the way to fetch the coroner, I wondered about it. Much of my own day had been "lost" to me. I remembered waking in a kind of mental fog, and could not recall such simple motions as getting out of bed to pee, dressing myself, or shaving. The only thing I remembered was finding myself at the window two or three times looking out at the twins. If I couldn't account for my actions, maybe Abby had lost track of time, too. Or maybe, I thought anxiously, she was right, and Regina no longer needed either of the girls to come through.

I slowed the horse two blocks in from the main street, stopping in front of a tall brick house with a shabby wooden porch. Ewing Eberhardt, the coroner, met me at the front door.

"Trouble over to Saunders's?" he asked, one hand lightly riding the door jamb. He knew me by sight—the result of the small town errands I'd run in Ruth's place over the last six months. His face said I was better known by reputation as the freakish twins' schoolmaster.

"Andrew," I nodded.

"Just give me a minute to get my bag and we'll go back together. You can tell me the details on the way."

"There's not much to it," I said.

129

He gave me a hard look, then disappeared down the dark throat of the hallway. I stayed on the porch mentally collecting the fragments of my scanty story.

He followed me to the buggy and as he climbed in on the opposite side, his black leather bag in hand, I saw something I'd never noticed about him before. He was missing the ring and pinky fingers of his left hand. Now with the sun winking off it, I saw that he wore his plain gold wedding ring on the right. Wing cleared his throat, waiting for me to begin. He was a quiet man given to slow, deliberate movements, and I wondered if he was continually compensating for whatever accident had cost him the missing flesh.

"Andrew's lying in his own bed," I said. "There's an empty bottle—"

"I know he was a drinker," Wing said, "but a man his age, you'd more likely find him tumbled at the bottom of his cellar steps." His eyes met mine again, and I found myself simultaneously wishing I'd thought of staging just such an accident and hoping my face hadn't registered the thought.

"He had cirrhosis—I'm sure of that."

Wing shrugged and went on. "Pretty hard to kill yourself drinking—even on a bender."

"Sometimes he fiddled with the drugs in his supply cabinet," I lied, suddenly pulling the syringe from my coat pocket and handing it over. "I didn't want the girls to catch on—it's bad enough as it is...."

The instant I mentioned the girls, I felt my blood pressure skyrocketing. What would Eberhardt think? No one knew we'd performed the surgery; worse, Andrew was dead, Ruth and Gabriel, gone. I felt my face going hot, red. I peeked to see if he was looking me over—

Wing merely eyed the syringe critically, sniffed around the glass plunger. "No smell of almonds; no smell at all, really. Colorless whatever it is," he said turning the syringe up to the light. "'Cept this drop of blood that's coagulated here, near the tip."

He indicated the place by running his finger up and down, but he was careful to maintain an invisible path more than a half inch away.

"Gener'lly speaking, people that inject themselves do it without drawing blood."

"If they're not drunk or clumsy with the drugs," I said. "And the needle's bent."

"Looks like somebody stepped on it." His face was as tight and unforgiving as a vise screwed close to the limit.

"I found it under Andrew's hand. He probably dropped it on the floor," I said, "when he lost consciousness."

He carefully folded a scrap of paper from a small leatherbound notebook around the bloody syringe, then he dropped it inside his medical bag. "We'll see," he said. "We'll see."

26

I watched Wing Eberhardt double the flesh-colored rubber tubes of his stethoscope and fold the contraption into his satchel. Andrew's corpse had taken on greater rigidity and his face was the color of a stage vampire in the glare of the gaslights.

I'd already watched him take Andrew's body temperature and he'd come prepared—not like what you'd expect from a semi-rural coroner—putting his hands on Andrew's knees or lower thighs to determine warmth or coolness. Eberhardt was more thorough than that; even making small incisions and inserting the probe of his thermometer into Andrew's organs.

"He's registering 78 degrees in the liver, fatty and packed in viscera as it is. That's pret' near to room temperature. He's been gone more than 14 hours is my guess," Wing said. He was hunting up and down Saunders's long body for the needle mark. "You told me he took drugs on occasion, injected himself. Never asked you or anybody else to do it. That right?" He gave out a small grunt.

"Yes," I said, glancing down at my folded hands and not knowing where else to look. I'd told him that Ruth and Gabriel had left for New Hampshire. Another alibi gone. "I've seen him glazed to the eyeballs, and I believe—"

"There's no signs of any puncture marks—new or old—here." Wing's eyes were focused in the unmarked innocent flesh of Andrew's elbow. "I'll just have a word with the twins, if you don't mind," Eberhardt said.

"They're just children—" I blurted out.

"All the same, I believe I'll see if they know something you don't."

I nodded miserably. I went to the doorway of Andrew's room. "Abby! Ellie!" I called, my voice echoing in the empty hallway.

Eberhardt looked at me then as if I'd gone round the bend. "What on earth are you callin' em for?" His face was flushed dark red with annoyance.

"I...you asked to talk—"

"And I'll go downstairs to the kitchen or the liberry or into the nursery. Man alive, think I'd make cripple girls walk to me, walk in the room where their father is lyin' dead?"

"Down here," Abby's voice rose from the depths of the library.

And I followed Wing Eberhardt down the stairs.

Ruth's words, *she can't come through unless they're separate,* roiled in my head. And yet, I thought to myself, this was Regina's scheming handiwork: The girls sat on a low hassock, arms about each other's waists. The irony wasn't lost on me: Even though Ellie's waist was twice the size of her sister's they'd managed to squeeze into the doubled green sack of the same velvet gown they'd worn the very first night I'd seen them. I found my eyes darting to the hem, but their feet were concealed. No one would've guessed Ellie was missing her left leg.

"Dr. Eberhardt," Abby said shyly, and she dipped her chin toward the boat shaped neckline Ruth had fashioned to accommodate two heads, two sets of shoulders when the girls had been attached.

"Young misses," Eberhardt nodded at the pair. "I guess you know your pa is passed on," he jerked his right thumb toward me.

"Mr. Granville told us," Ellie whispered. She took a hanky she'd been clotting into sticky white dough inside her fist and dabbed her eyes. "What happened?" she asked, and when she raised one brow, I saw Regina—the goddamn bitch, the double goddamned bitch—slyly peeping out from the girl's face. I saw her dark jade eyes leering out beneath the fringe of Ellie's pale pinkish lashes.

Eberhardt's hands were on his hips. His eye swept over Ellie's protruding belly, and I saw—as clearly as if he'd said it out loud—that the word motive had just clicked into place in his mind.

I knew in that moment I was lost, I knew Abby was lost, Regina was in control. Ewing Eberhardt was a bright man but he was a country coroner, and there was nothing in his experience—in his concept of what could or might be—that would ever let him see what was really happening.

Her arm tightened about her daughter's waist, the fingers squeezing the soft flesh I so wanted to caress gently, the force of her demon's mind squeezing the words down the child's throat, and I heard Regina Cahill Saunders speak again.

"We're orphans now. Ruth's gone. And Gabriel. Who'll take care of all of us? Who?"

I saw Wing blanch. "There, there, Miss Ellie," he said.

"The wake, the funeral, what'll we do? What'll we do?" Abby began to rock and moan.

"Was it the drink?" Regina asked slyly through Ellie's puffy red lips. "He liked his liquor of a night," she said.

It would've taken a stronger man than Ewing Eberhardt to tell a twelve-year-old girl the facts. He couldn't do it. And whatever his suspicions about me—and I was sure they ran deep—he wasn't going to tell the girl her father's murderer was standing free and easy in the family drawing room.

"There'll be an inquest. That's the usual...when a man of 48 is found...in his own bed. It won't be me doing the tests—everything I collected will be sent on to Albany. They've got the proper equipment to investigate all possibilities." His brown eyes lit on me, but he left the rest unsaid. Then he went on. "I've covered Andrew with the bedsheets, and I'll call in John Madison and Sons to wake him."

"They're best? We'd want the best," Abby said, staring at her hands in her lap.

"We were so young...we can't remember...when mother died...." And here the false Ellie snatched at her sister's unsteady hand and clenched it tightly in her own. "You see, Dr. Eberhardt, we don't even know who our family uses—for this kind of thing."

"I'll call John Madison," Eberhardt said again.

And in my mind's eye I saw two scenes simultaneously. The rough hewn planks of the gallows, a black cotton hood fitted with a jerk over my head, and the heavy canvas fabric of a dirty white strait jacket scratching the exposed flesh of my chin. My arms were painfully secured in opposing directions, a stream of yellow urine poured down my inner thigh.

I heard a snorting sound erupting out of my mouth and nose. It was inexplicable to them, I knew, but I was hysterical. I would be accused of murdering Andrew, I was certain of that. There were only two roads out of Hyde Park, New York for me. Death or prison. I began to laugh.

Gabriel's telegram came the day before the funeral:

Ruth failing fast. deepest regrets for girls' sorrow, But impossible for me to come.

DISSOLUTION

"We do not die—only sleep a while, wait for judgment"

I wondered who the last line referred to—Ruth? Andrew? Regina? It didn't matter, he was my last hope and he would not be there to take up for me. The autopsy confirmed that Andrew's liver was riddled with cirrhosis. But it was the massive overdose of morphine that killed him. There was no point in delaying the burial; with the facts in, Ewing Eberhardt felt he could afford to postpone the inquest a day or two.

I knew I had to act quickly, but I had no idea what action to take. Should I leave? Fleeing would only make me look guilty. But if I did, should I go alone or take one or both girls with me? Would Ruth's warning come true, would I be ferrying Regina out of the house, a stowaway concealed deep inside Ellie's or Abby's mind?

In a small town gossip spreads more quickly than a grease fire. I was trained to observe closely, I would watch how the mourners acted around me. Then my thoughts broke off except for the obsessive round that was like the hollow peal of a death gong: The funeral will tell. Andrew's funeral will tell.

27

The day before the wake John Madison and Sons laid Andrew's corpse out in the library. I went in to introduce myself.

"Granville." Madison Senior, a stout fiftyish man built like a cistern, bowed. He was civil, but distant.

There was only one son in the firm apparently. Young John. He was about my own age, knobby and thin. His chief duty seemed to be to look properly tragic and to hide a set of overlapped and slightly crossed front teeth behind lips that were pressed in a grim line.

"You'll excuse us now," Madison Senior intoned, shutting me out, banging the doors closed to get on with his work.

I told myself to calm down, to keep paranoia at bay, and watched surreptitiously from a crack in the double doors as they arranged Andrew in his mahogany casket. The rigor mortis had left the body; they were washing the flaccid skin with alcohol swabs.

"Do you think he did it?" Young John asked. "Eberhardt was right—there's no marks."

"Never jump to conclusions—it doesn't do in this business," the elder sniffed, unfolding Andrew's arms from his chest. Still, I saw his eyes riveted on the delicate inner crease of the elbow.

I didn't want to hear any more, and I crept away.

After they left I went into the semi-darkened room. Andrew was wearing a starched shirt, his best black cutaway coat. I guessed it was Madison himself who powdered the face, applied the pancake make-up, brushed the thinning hair. They'd inserted a gardenia in the buttonhole of his suit, but the scent of the funeral flowers—lilies, tuberoses, violets—was overpowering.

I found myself standing by the casket, staring at the little details. The stitching on the cuff of his jacket, the tufted blue upholstery Saunders lay on. His shoes—shiny patent leather evening slippers—were incongruously made for dancing.

I let my fingers curl over the edge of the wood.

Suddenly I smelled the heavy musk of sherry—as if the corpse had been drinking at its own funeral party.

Perhaps formaldehyde smelled more like alcohol than I realized.

I bent, intending to sniff gardenia.

Instead I felt a warm puff of air gently brushing my forehead and my right cheek. A cloud of sweet wine assailed me and I drew back in confusion. Could one ghost create another? No, it couldn't be. He was dead! That smell—it was from the chemicals!

"He wasn't embalmed," Ellie said.

I started at her voice, turned, staring through the open doors at taunting green eyes. She stared back.

Then, clumsily, Ellie wheeled herself down the hall.

28

"**S**tuart," Abby cried out, "Stuart!" she called again. It was perhaps two in the morning. I'd gone to bed with nothing resolved in my mind, but I told myself here at least was something I might follow through with, one thing I might be good at: comforting a child down with the nightmare.

"She came to me," Abby wept when I went in to ssh her. "In my dreams—oh God, Stuart she crept right in while I was sleeping and took me the way I'd pick up a ragdoll until I had no will and there was nothing of me at all."

Abby was crying hard, her hand slipped out from the blankets and her fingers stole into mine. "Why? Why does she do it? How can she do it, if I don't want her to?" Now the child's hand withdrew and she made a fist, pummeling it against her drawn up knee.

Abby was alone in the nursery. The wide empty bed, her wavy hair hanging down made her look younger, more innocent. "Maybe at first I wished she'd come," Abby said, her voice thick with tears, "but I don't now and here she is—sucking up my soul."

"I've thought about it," I said. My hand went to her girl's bony arm. "I've thought about it late in the night, trying to understand same as you." I paused. "She's cancer, Abby. She's a cancer."

Abby's eyes looked deeply into mine. I saw the question lurking in her wide-eyed stare and I went on. "Cancer—it's a kind of madness—not of the mind—but of the physical self. Do you know why?"

"No," she shook her head, the strands of hair undulating gently over her upturned knees.

"Because it runs amok and doesn't know when to stop. Cancer—it can only live because it has a host in healthy cells. Yet every time it multiplies, it destroys. But it's so mindless, it doesn't care and it'll keep on going 'til all the healthy tissue— 'til the very body that supports it—is eaten away and cannot live," I said.

Abby looked up, uncomprehending, her tiny knot of a chin with its heartbreaking cleft tilted up at me.

"Don't you see what I mean?"

"No," she said. I saw her china blue eyes brim, the whites going the silver bright of a mirror.

"Look here," I said, thinking medical terms were beyond her. I would appeal to her imagination, but because I knew what I had to say would terrify her, I let my hand steal out to lightly caress the soft filaments of red hair, and to touch— ever so gently—the whitened brow. "I've done some reading about demons, possession."

She gasped—a hard short intake of breath, and now her hand, unwittingly I was sure, fluttered and lit on the bony cap of my knee. "Demons," she said.

"The thing about the undead—they're just like cancer. They'll go on taking from the host, getting stronger and stronger."

Her hand grazed my knee again, I couldn't look at her. "They're driven same as disease—so stupid, mindless they don't seem to realize if they kill what keeps them alive, they die too. All that matters to these demons is control, winning. They don't see the human side at all—that winning is really losing."

"Lost," she breathed. "Only one can live, only one can be chosen." Her hand fell away, her head and shoulders slumped downward.

And I saw that my words, like the cruelest of knives, sank inside the tender flesh of her understanding.

"Oh my God, Stuart, what can we do?"

Now, her hands clasped my wrist painfully, moving in opposite directions like those of a widow woman watching a stage melodrama and hanging mindlessly onto the velvet-clad bar in the first row of the balcony.

"Abby, you're hurting my skin."

"Oh, I've given you an Indian burn." The hands flew off my thick wrist. "Sorry."

I nodded.

"But what'll we do?"

Without meaning to, I spoke my thought aloud. "Ruth said your mother was able to come back because you two were separated."

A light dawned in her eyes, her words came in a slow stammer. "Then—then you must do the surgery, beloved," she said, her eyes peering into the depths of mine.

"Surgery—"

"No one knows we've been separated. I've been thinking about what Ellie said. She's right. They'll accuse you of my father's murder. But if we...if we're reattached and Ellie and I are one, then my mother can't intervene."

"What are you saying? Abby, it will be the worse for me!" I shouted, panic rising inside me. "If they believe you two can't move about and are cripples, there is no other conclusion! That only leaves me to have done it! Don't you see, even if one of you was known to hate him—-to despise him, wish him in his grave a thousand times a thousand days over—together, attached—she'd have to convince her sister to carry out the deed! Two in tandem." I held up my two fingers locked along the vertical of the knuckles. "All right, one might be mad, one might be vengeful—but two! It would take the two of you to carry out the crime!" I'd slipped to my knees and now my big head was buried between her slight thighs, and I felt her hands moving through the thatch of my hair.

"In your own way you're telling me because of the amputation they might think it was Ellie—"

"Regina had control, but it was her!"

"Are you protecting me, or yourself?"

"Both," I cried.

"Ssh, we have now."

"Now," I said, turning my own tear-streaked face up to hers.

"Yes, we have this moment." She paused. "But afterwards, you've got to take Ellie..."

"Take her—"

"Stuart," she pleaded, "it's her only chance...."

"But you don't make sense," I said. "How will taking Ellie prevent Regina from breaking though?" I got up to pace. "You said maybe she doesn't even need you—either of you—to come through!"

"I was wrong. She might not need our willingness or consent, but she needs a body. I have your love. And I'm afraid for Ellie, because if I can't control her—"

"Please." I stopped, took her hands in mine. "Forget this...so-called surgery. Let's just leave, go away—you and me."

She lifted her head, her eyes were bright. Her voice was the strongest, bravest thing I ever heard. Soft and resigned, it went to a place I could not understand with any part of my fallen mind, my guilt-tortured soul.

"No. Because I see the surgery now in a way that defies the sense, the logic of the thing, but I know in my soul it has to be done—the same way I know the bluebird that makes its nest every spring in yonder apple tree."

I'd caught the word—it was one of my own, and even if I was in country New York, 'yonder' was not a term of that place or time. I only fell into using it when my accent slipped through drink or fatigue—still, Abby had usurped my southernism.

I smiled, felt my eyes crinkling at the corners to show my pleasure at this small token of her love and esteem, but before I could comment, she went on, holding her small hand up to stop me from breaking in on her determined mood.

"I do love you, Stuart. And I know you have to reattach me and Ellie."

My mind went blank. It was as if someone had told me I must go down to Andrew's cabinet, fill a syringe with a lethal dose of opium and put it into her. I couldn't get it straight; no, I could not do it.

"It's the only way," she said, her voice barely audible.

"You say I must do a surgery that is anathema to me." I turned on her. "Do you know you're asking me to go against everything I believe in, everything that was ever a dream to me?" I put my hands on my hips. I was suddenly furious. "Yes." I shrieked, "*Yes!* I almost threw it completely away for absinthe and liquor in piano bars and the sleezy red lace that covered the white limbs on the whores in New Orleans." I knocked my fist against the center of my chest: "But that doesn't make the dream of being a doctor—a healer!—less real. It doesn't! Abby, however I hurt myself, whatever I did wrong—it doesn't make my dream less real!

"I came here because I thought there was a speck of a chance I could salvage what was left of that dream and find myself!

"I cannot do what you are asking—not even if Regina swoops down on me like some wild harpy and kills me tonight."

"She won't." Abby began to cry. "She won't because that would be too quick and easy and she needs your suffering."

Our eyes locked, and Abby suddenly raised her slim, hairless arms towards me.

"Hold me, Stuart," she whispered.

Her breasts were the merest buds; her child's round belly was only beginning to flatten, to be drawn smooth by the slight adolescent flare in her hips. I gazed at her, and I saw a face that was caught between the dreams of girlish youth and womanhood.

And God help me it was her innocence that spoke to me.

I took her with the part of me that was man enough to be slow and gentle and sweet. I told myself I was Poe with his Virginia.

Let them kill me for that crime, I thought.

I took her.

And we both loved it.

"Ewing Eberhardt's evidence is going to send you the gallows," Abby said. "I know Ellie loves you. It's such a little thing, my darling."

Abby's small hand crushed the flesh between my jaw bone and my temple. It was not her touch—that was featherlight. It was the tingling sensation of her fingers sweeping over my flesh with tenderness and love—that was crush enough for me.

"How can I?"

"Because I ask it, because you must."

I was young in those days, so instead of giving myself over again immediately to my beloved, I trusted I would have stamina enough later.

I wiped the dampness from between my legs with a crusty towel, and I went to the room down the hall where her sister slept.

I woke her, saw those blue eyes fill with something like the hope of the world.

I lay down next to her; at the same instant I felt Regina breaking through, and it was hers—the adult body I made love to for the second time that night. I heard her moans when my tongue pressed deep inside her. I felt her woman's wet damping my chin in the hard crinkly curls of her pubes.

It was Regina—and yet whenever I happened to look up from the business I cared not a damn about, I'd have sworn, it was a child's adoring blue eyes I looked into.

"You chose me," she whispered, her swollen crippled body pressing against mine. "You love me."

I did not have the heart to tell her it was her sister's love that brought me to her bed, her sister's wish that for this one and only time Ellie would have what she wanted.

So, in a way I do not understand even to this day, I satisfied all three women and myself.

I came back to sleep with Abby; wanting no more than to feel her slight weight lying in my weary arms. But the minute I skinned back the covers to lie next to her, her small palm was mashing the curls in the center of my chest above my solar plexus.

"No—you have to get up."

"Abby, I'm dead dog weary, and all I want to do is crawl between clean sheets."

"Tomorrow is the funeral."

"Uh huh," I said, fatigue making my eyelids droop half mast. "And that sonofabitch, Eberhardt will be measuring my hide for just the right size trophy to span his chimney piece."

My head was crashed into the pillow; it was so late at night I could feel my beard stubble scraping the soft cotton of the pillow slip. I began to drift downwards, skimming the edges of that dozy, pre-sleep state.

"Wake up! You have to hurry while she's still inside Ellie!"

I felt Abby shaking me hard.

"Now, Stuart! You have to do the surgery now while the demon sleeps!"

29

You will think I'm mad—utterly mad—and that without knowing for sure, I might have taken my chances with Wing Eberhardt and his evidence against me. Ruth would have defended me—and foolishly optimistic as that might sound, there were people who respected Ruth. Even if she'd supposedly taken carnal advantage of teenage girls, it had been a long time ago, and some of them believed the charges had been trumped up. Gabriel had a reputation for a steady head, all those years of marriage counted. Ruth was a good woman. I had no doubts about her innocence.

All of those are true things, but the most compelling truth was what I told Abby: Regina was a cancer, and there was no stopping her anymore.

I believed then, I was going to face the hangman's noose. It was the preferred method of execution in New York until they built Sing Sing and decided juicing a man 'til his brains boiled out his ears was a better way to kill.

I went into the small room where Ellie slept. It was dark, and I had to grope blindly, my left hand riding the cool plaster of the walls. In my right I carried a syringe—the same sort Regina had filled with morphine to kill Andrew. But inside this brittle glass tube was a scant centimeter of valium. I drew my arm back, then plunged it lightly and delicately as I could into the second large vein on the back of Ellie's left hand.

She started to cry out—I saw her lips draw back in a rictus—but the drug shut her down. Then I gathered her thick, bee-shaped body—the midriff bloated, her live leg still stick thin and spindly—into my arms.

And silently, my feet making no sound, I carried her into what had been Andrew's office.

30

I tilted my head back and took a long swallow from the dark green bottle, set it on the floor behind my tottery legs, then wiped my mouth.

Before I could adjust the gas lamps and get Ellie properly prepped, I heard Abby's light barefoot tread just beyond the door.

She was wearing a white, long-sleeved cotton nightdress with delicate ruching around the throat and tiny pin tucks—like the bib on a tuxedo shirt—across the bosom.

Her large round eyes met mine. She crossed the threshold, and before I could utter a word, she was slowly and methodically hoisting herself onto the makeshift operating table that had served us too well in the past year. She slid her bottom across the crisp ground sheet, answered my unspoken thought.

"You have to do it now, because tomorrow my father will be buried. And after that—"

I cut her off. "He'll be buried in any case."

There was no denying the drink had gone to my head. I took another swig. Ease the pain, it's more than any man can bear, Stuart, I droned inwardly.

I upended the bottle, which was one of the last three the doctor had left in his cellar. Not fifteen minutes earlier, I'd gathered up all I saw after lurching down the open wooden slats that served as steps. Now, in the office, I was not drinking champagne or brandy or even a bottle of something common like gin or whisky. The stuff I tippled, feeling the warm brown liquid course down my chin—and Christ I licked those drops—was from a bottle of Sicilian Arini. The cork was sealed in ancient black wax and a tiny metal cage, jammed so tight and hard against the long green neck, I'd nicked the skin on my thumb trying to get past it. The liquor was as sweet as the scuppernong I'd grown up with and twice as potent.

"It's Regina making you drink like that," Abby said.

"What do you know about it?"

"I know what she did to my father. She made him drink. I see what she's doing to you—"

"Eh, you say, you say." I sat back, convinced I was aiming for the seatback—but my buttocks missed Andrew's stiff-staved barrel of a chair by half a foot. The castors shot out from under my lumbering body.

"I say you have *no* choice: unless you reattach us, you're a lost man, and there's no going back—not ever." She lay back on the operating table.

My mind was clouded with liquor and regret. I didn't understand, but I believe in that moment I loved her more than ever I'd thought possible.

Abby seemed to read my mind.

"You drunken ass—you said it yourself—she can't come through if we're attached! Ruth knew it!"

Ruth.

I heard her quiet voice suddenly cutting through the haze in my brain. *You got to keep a lid on your fears and suspicions, Stuart....*

I stood up, moved toward the supply cabinet. I reached for the glass knob on the door, then stopped, pressing an unsteady hand up to an already aching brow. "I can't do this!"

"Please," Abby said. "They'll take you away—no matter what happens to me and Ellie. You're going to your death or to jail. But I'm *still* a child and I will not live whatever life I have in her shadow. I cannot be my mother's prisoner...not now, not anymore. The next time she comes through, it will be forever! Please, if you love me...save me, save us both," she said.

It will be up to you to bring the two of them together, Stuart. The hired woman's voice echoed in my head. *I had to learn to love my girls in a different way....*

I think Ruth meant as if they were her own, as if they had no infirmity. But I couldn't make my mind fit around the confusion. "Ssh," I said aloud, returning to the operating table. "Ssh."

I was sobbing, cold tears burning my cheeks, when I lowered the ether-soaked flannel against her face.

My mind went back to the first surgery: Andrew's fierce gray eyes looming over his white mask, the smell of blood, the sound of the metallic saw blade rasping against the thick bridge of bone.

Now of course, I was alone, and the 'reattachment' would consist of simply sewing them together skin to skin— like pelts placed side by side in a fur piece.

If that surgery was brilliant, the kind that broke new ground, this was simple scut work. Ellie's missing leg dictated they would be joined as they were before—Abby on the left, her right leg inward to compensate for the amputation.

I undressed them, swabbed the surgical sites with mercurochrome.

They lay unmoving, as pale and still under the harsh light as the waxy figures in the death tableau of a Renaissance painting.

For one brief instant, I smelled sherry in the cool air and I shuddered. I put the thought of specters and apparitions out of my mind. No, I told myself, it was only my own liquor-drenched breath behind the mask.

I inhaled deeply, cleared my mind in order to visualize the incisions: The first, from just below the ribs down; next I would make a series of transverse cuts across each abdomen and buttocks. Then, when I was sure there was an adequate blood supply, I would peel the "skin flaps" back and attach each to the opposite twin.

I injected Abby with a combination of valium and morphine, I plied both her and Ellie with more ether, and taking a deep breath, I began.

31

It was a blood bath. Whether it was because I was working alone, or because my mind was both conflicted and addled with drinking—it was a mess right from the start.

I sponged and sponged away the fast-welling blood that bubbled like red oil out of Ellie's side, obscuring my sight of muscle and tissues, of the gaping wound itself—

"Oh piss in the moonshine!" I shouted, working at top speed. "Dammit, stop bleeding" I shoved a metal hemostat inside her blindly, then another and another, until they hung out of her like long silver leeches.

My skull was throbbing. Her blood pulsed in steady rhythmic wavelets over my gloved fingers. I probed; clamped again, snapping the jaws of the instrument shut in frustration.

"Oh, fuck me," I said.

"That's what we all want, Stuart."

A sigh.

I stopped, puzzled.

Giggling.

Abby's lids fluttered briefly, a sinister cat-smile twitched across her lips, she opened her eyes, and Regina sat up.

Except, except, my mind whirled, it was not exactly Regina. The body was Abby's, but the eyes looking at me were the sharp green of polar ice. I stepped back in confusion, shut my eyes, raised my hands, the blood-slimed fingers covering my face. "No," I whispered. "She can't be—"

"Ah, bright lad, I knew you'd understand," Regina said. She rolled on her side, snapped her fingers, idly flicking a pill of invisible lint from the bottom sheet.

The voice was husky, thick with seduction. I smelled violets—but the scent was sour now—as if they'd rotted in the dark of an abandoned hothouse. "Abby—"

"Call me that if you want—in fact, I expect you to. After all, everyone else will." She laughed, then spun herself off the table. Naked, she gave a slight twirl. "Whatever shall I wear to Father's funeral tomorrow," she said, propping one childishly shaped finger under her chin. The voice was an imitation of a girl's—and close enough to fool outsiders. "I haven't any black, do you suppossse," she lisped faintly, "mauve will be all right?" Then she tilted her head back, the great mass of red hair hanging down her back, and gave out a throaty laugh.

"Stop it, stop it!" I screamed. I lunged forward, seized her narrow shoulders, felt the pads of my fingers sinking deep in her flesh.

"Stop what, Stuart," she jerked herself away from me, then rubbed her upper left arm. There were red marks from my fingers that would turn blackish blue. "I'm not going to stop anything," Regina said. She glared at me, her eyes hot, phosphorescent like a poisonous fungus glowing in a jungle. "Don't delude yourself that when the ether wears off, your precious Abby will return." She paused. "There is no Abby— not any more. Have you forgotten what they told you?" She snicked her head toward Ellie's sprawled body, "Only one can live, only one will be chosen—"

I gave a gasp, my eyes moving in frenzied arcs staring at her, at Ellie.

"And do you think I'd choose to live out my days inside a mutilated cripple? Your child is in me," she passed the flat of her hand over the tiny mound of childish belly.

"But, Ellie is—"

She cut me off. "Ever hear of pseudocyesis, hmmmm, Doctor Granville? Never saw a hysterical pregnancy, I suppose," she said. "Such a pity you didn't study obstetrics before you were pitched out of medical school."

I had though. I pivoted my head slowly, heard the tendons creaking in my neck. Ellie's abdomen had a deflated look—like a squishy balloon with its air slowly leaking out. Printed words spiraled up at me: *Usually seen in abnormal mental states. Prevalent when the young woman desires or imagines she has had sexual intercourse with a man she wants as a lover or husband. Under anesthesia the enlargement of the abdomen disappears.*

"I'd say a crippled girl with a crush who's infatuated herself and jealous of her identical twin's romance with their tutor qualifies in spades—wouldn't you?"

She was reading my mind again. I went to Ellie's torn body. The bleeding had slowed to a light trickle—not a great deal more than you'd see if you pricked your finger on a sewing needle. But the long ragged cut I'd made haunted me. "It was you, wasn't it? You pretended to be Abby, pretended to want the surgery. Tell me why, goddamn you!" I whirled on her, my arm swung back ready to strike.

"Look at the time, Stuart," she said rising on her toes. "You'll never finish before they come!"

The windows were covered with wooden shutters, put up I'd always supposed, for the sake of a patient's privacy in the days when Andrew Saunders might have been optimistic about having a regular practice. Now I saw golden light glowing around the thin edges of the slats.

"You better hurry. It's nearly eight in the morning," she said, and I heard the hall clock chiming the three quarter hour. Her laughter made a tinkling sound around the saccharin notes. She rose higher on her toes—looking for all the world like some diminutive version of a fairy godmother in a tale. I thought dreamily, this is a demonic version, a story that runs in reverse, so now she'll dash from the room, disappear, run up the stairs to dress for the funeral. Instead, she sprinted forward and seized the nearest scalpel from the sterile tray.

"No!" I screamed.

Before I could stop her, she made a long gash that was the twin of the one I'd carved into Ellie. Then she slashed again and again, across her belly. The knife flickered and descended behind the crest of her hip. Blood poured down her thighs, the blade fell from her fingers, she swayed.

Andrew's plaintive voice wailed in my head, *she's bleeding, she's bleeding.*

I gathered her up, hoisted her onto the table, and feverishly, like a man possessed I set about sewing up the wounds—first hers, then Ellie's.

32

When the clock struck nine that was how they found me. It was John Madison coming early to oversee last minute details before Andrew's wake.

I never heard his knock, never heard anything 'til the doors slid open and he was teetering on the threshold, gasping with shock. His oldest son stood just behind his father's black serge-clothed elbow, his mouth open to reveal his crossed teeth.

"Stay back, Johnny," the undertaker warned, his hand pistoning backwards to halt his son. "The man is mad," he said.

"I know what it looks like," I said helplessly. All of us were drawn to gaze at the girls' slight bodies, nude and seemingly hacked apart, lying on the table.

"They wanted to be...together again...I didn't want to do it. I started to—but I didn't, and I was just now...now closing them up. Finishing. It took longer than I thought. I didn't want them badly scarred if I could help it, you see."

I gestured with the scalpel waving it slowly over them. I turned and tried to smile. The muscles in my face felt all wrong, hitching this way and that—as if I were leering, maybe. I was aware of the dried blood smearing my cheeks. "Mr. Madison," I began—

"I think she's dead," Johnny said, pointing at Eleanor.

159

"Go get Eberhardt," the undertaker said to his son. "Now! Tell him to bring his bag, have his wife send for the ambulance."

The boy rushed from the room.

"Get away from that table," Madison said.

I sat down, hard, in Andrew's chair, there was nothing to do but stare at my own gloved and bloodied hands.

EPILOGUE

There is not much to do in this place; there is very little to see. They say that isolation is good for the imagination—I do not find it so. Or perhaps, it's because I never had one—or the one I had was insufficiently developed, bogged down by liquor and guilt.

Looking back now, I suppose it was the failure of my imagination that led to my downfall. If I'd been able to accept Regina in the guise of my beloved Abby, I might have lived out my days happy. Crazy, perhaps...but undoubtedly content. And would it have mattered in that household where no one ever came?

And if I'd been willing to accept the situation, I'd be with her. She was right in the end—it doesn't matter if you call her Abby or Regina.

Instead, I tried to hold on to sanity, save the girl, do right by her. Now I have nothing. Except the pulsing walls of my own brain. In this place (and let me assure you the Doctor—Doctor Williams—is both bright and knowing) I'm called a madman. Locked away, my dinner comes cut up on a tray divided into neat two inch square spaces on the Bakelite: potatoes, peas, cubes of meat (no knives for me, haha) apple cobbler.

The staff is small and overworked; it's easier for them to dress me in rubber pants. A snip of a girl who has yet to see her nineteenth year shaves me weekly.

I was a trained surgeon and mad. Now I am being rehabilitated toward sanity. I can sing all of the Ivory soap flake jingle from the radio. I string beads, name the colors—blue, yellow, green, clear, red.

"Do you know why you're here?"

The doctor had a Viennese beard.

My head was shaved like a convict's.

I lay on the railed bed, my wrists and legs restrained with thick leather straps. His face was close to mine. I smelled his lunch—cheese, boiled beef and red wine.

"Andrew, Dr. Saunders..." I began.

"No," he corrected, moving into stride. "That was never proven—to a certainty. His fingerprints were on the syringe. He might, after all, have committed suicide. Despondent, perhaps, on discovering the tutor he hired raped both and impregnated one of his daughters." His hands were clasped behind his back, he paused thoughtfully. "Saunders was a genius after all—that surgery proved it. Brilliant men are subject to fits of depression."

"He was a drunk," I said through gritted teeth.

"He indulged, certainly," Doctor Williams nodded crisply. "But the fact is—he wasn't incapacitated, he wasn't a dipsomaniac," he sniffed. "Never could have held himself together for that operation, otherwise." He leaned over the bed.

"On the other hand, Mister Granville, you amputated a young girl's leg. You tortured her, then tried to cover up the crime of rape by performing a quack surgery. What did you think? That no would suspect you of fucking freaks?" He glared at me.

"It wasn't like that." I stared at the ceiling. One crack looked like a broken champagne glass, the goblet halved and jagged over the straight stem.

"Bit of a dipsomaniac yourself—they found you drunk, bottles strewn about Dr. Saunders' office."

"I drank, yes." I squinted, angled my head right. Now the crack was a pig's head and snout, stuck on a stick.

"Do you remember trying to reattach them?"

"Vaguely," I lied.

"I have it on the best authority you also tried to induce an abortion in Abigail Saunders."

"Andrew did the same to Regina," I muttered. The doctor, warmed to his subject, seemed not to hear. Regina had her revenge against Andrew at last, I thought.

"And further, you attempted some half-assed version of curettage on Eleanor Saunders—perforating her uterus in the process. You let that girl bleed to death, and she was not even pregnant." "

"Ewing Eberhardt saw—"

He shouted me down. "Eberhardt admitted he couldn't tell one twin from the other! They found your semen! You terrorized those children by raping them repeatedly. You cut off Ellie's leg when she tried to run away! Abby told us how you forced them to pretend they were still attached when the coroner came!" He stopped, put his face close to mine. His brown eyes glittered. "That is what the evidence showed, that is what the judge ruled. That is why you're here. I would make an effort to remember it, Mr. Granville. The sooner you remember, the better. Understand?"

I understood that one ghost can spawn another, that Andrew had been there at the end, that I was the actor in a reprise, playing out a tragic scene for the second time. Ruth had tried to warn me. Regina and Andrew. Spirits stuffed with evil, condemned to the same dull round for eternity.

Except, it wasn't their hell—it was mine.

I saw her once years ago, it was February, 1894; and it was only a quick glance through the mesh on the window. Fool that I was, I actually tried to rub the misty condensation from the glass behind the wirework.

Her carriage was parked in the oval just beyond the grounds. She was coming through the tall verdigris gate, her tiny hands muffed in brown sealskin, a long cape. Even at that distance I could see she was full blown, big with the child. The living proof of my madness brought directly to the doctor's own doorstep.

There was someone with her—a man, mincing his steps to match her pace. I believe it was Gabriel. I don't know.

Her skin was pale, but rouged at the cheeks by the wind and cold. The reddish curls peeked from under the heavy hood. She looked like an angel. "Abby, Abby," I called.

A bride, a girl.

"Abby! Please," I shouted.

She looked up at me, green eyes lit with seductive mirth. Lips parted in a half smile to show she approved of my keeping her secret. The blue-eyed girl that was Abby was gone forever.

No one remembers the color of a freak's eyes—they are too busy not looking at the confusion of arms and legs and the crude fabric tent that serves the joined body as a covering.

The man that I thought might be Gabriel kept his face down. I was certain his eyes were gray, and the smell of Sherry hung round his narrow mouth. But Regina winked at me, then lifted her skirts daintily and began to climb the front porch steps. She had escaped, as Ruth said she might, at last.

Groaning, I tapped the glass, then banged at it with the flat of my hand until they led me away.

**Matteawan State Hospital
for the Criminally Insane
June 10, 1933**

THE SHEILA NA GIG

Tab.VI. p.36.

Tſiovanna Areli.

Gul-Badſamır:

1

"**H**ey! You! Goddamn brute!"

Tom Smith woke shivering inside the ship's belly. He'd been dreaming that Pitcher, his fat calico had been sitting on his chest and breathing mice and dust smells into his face, the old tom's claws kneading the boy's thin ribs. Now, he sat up dreamily, only half aware that the rough brown hop sack he was using as a blanket was no longer scratching the tender skin under his throat. The narrow, smelly hold was lit by a rough nub of candle, and what he saw was that his erstwhile bunkmate, Jack Cahill, had one arm cocked back, the second of a pair of heavy cracked brogans in hand and ready to aim.

He followed Jack's steady gaze: the filament of a thin translucent whisker peeked from a jagged hole in the planking that was only the size of a six pence.

"Bastard! Jack shrieked, and hurled the boot at the rat. There was the sharp sound of shoe leather striking wood, followed by a muffled squeal and the sound of scrabbling feet.

Jack smiled, showing brownish teeth.

167

"Sorry for the rah-hoo, laddie, but he was on your chest—large as life. Christ, I hate 'em."

Tom nodded, uncertain what to say. Terrible as his life had been back in county Meath, rats were certainly more than he was used to—but then, so was Jack.

"I always heard rats'll suck a baby's breath," Tom said cautiously.

"Don't mind what your old Gran said, lad." Jack lay back, his spade of a chin turned upward. "Just think: New York the day after next. Europe's a dead whore, but America's a virgin twitch," Jack winked. "An' they say her very cunt runs with gold."

That word, Tom thought, flinching. He made himself push away the mental image of his father's scrawled writing, the crumpled parchment page spattered with ink and blood. Out loud he said, "My father said I might make a new start."

"That's the spirit," Jack said, turning on his stomach abruptly and punching up the north end of his rag bundle to make a sort of pillow.

But of course Jack didn't really know what he'd been through. The cruel things Granny Rose had done to him, to Delia and Ellen; and if he'd retaliated it wasn't his fault, Tom thought. He'd been driven to it. In his mind's eye, he saw Granny's little paring knife skating toward him, the curved blade glinting. In the semi-dark, he lightly skimmed his fingers over his manhood. It was intact. Relief flooded through him.

For a brief instant Tom saw the fire—the whitewashed cottage burning with a fierce flame like a cotton ball soaked in oil, his grandmother's wicked staring eyes draining from the sockets like rotten grapes. He shut this picture out of his mind, too.

"Half of Ireland must be on this ship," Jack said.

It wasn't anything Tom's own mother hadn't said the last ten or more years. He thought of the lean decade on the farm his father had optimistically christened "Pink Cloud." Forty acres, most of it bog, but the old man been hopeful, hard working back then—or so his Mother said. Optimism my arsehole, his granny Rose taunted Cedric.

"My Dad always said there's big money to be made when a country like the U.S. is on the brink of war," Jack said. "Opportunity and time for any man with gumption to turn his life around." His hands were locked behind his head, he was gazing at the low ceiling of the hold, his lean body swaying—just perceptibly—with the slow rock of the waves slapping the boat.

"Mine too." Why had he said that? Cedric barely knew Ireland was out of Druid times. Didn't Tom have three dead brothers named Patrick buried in the family plot?

"I'll be forty come spring." Jack sat up, felt in his pack for the gin bottle and uncorked it. He took a swig, and held it toward Tom.

Tom sipped out of politeness and handed it back. He was aware of the older man's graying beard stubble, the smell of sweat coming off his body. Part of his fifteen year old mind admired Jack's spunk; part was terrified. Only the worst failure of a man would have flashed a pitiful pound note or two and bribed the steward—as he himself had done, twelve days earlier—for passage on a ship.

"You can always remake your life, lad—no matter what it's been, and that's God's own truth," he said popping the cork back on.

Tom agreed. But on the whole, he was glad when the older man blew out the light and the hold was plunged into darkness.

But the dreams, the hideous memories of the last three years took him—a lonely friendless boy—down deeper, anyway.

"They made Brigantia a saint."

Tom looked up from the bench where he was polishing his brother Bob's boots. His grandmother had a wild, faraway look in her brown eyes. She was huddled near the fireplace with a bowl of milk and bread in her lap.

"The stupid Irish, they made Brigantia a saint!" Rose Smith said again.

Tom knew she might go on with this—or another equally meaningless phrase—for hours. He skinned the bristle brush against the leather instep and gave out a sigh.

"Tom," Cedric said. "Show some respect for the aged." He rustled in the drift of manuscript pages—most of them halved scraps—that covered his desk. "What does it matter if she prattles a bit? She can't help it."

"Right." He left off shoe blacking and got up. But it did matter, Tom thought, because his father was spouting a lie. Cedric urging tolerance of his grandmother had nothing to do with respect and everything to do with his own motives. Rose was said—not by the family, but by the local farmers and their wives—to be a hag, a witch. Cedric liked to hear her talk because in some way, Tom knew, his father secretly believed she would come out of her mania and empower his failed writing, set right the wreck of his life.

He's just waiting for a chair to fly across the room so he can put it in his bloody book. Tom didn't know if Cedric felt his mother leant atmosphere or just spurred a flagging imagination, and he didn't care. What he did care about was the way the snarly-haired old woman gave him the flits.

Tom glanced at her. Her head was canted sideways, her wrinkled mouth, dripping milk. She was staring at him; then her tongue flicked out and she licked the warm milk from the corner of her mouth. She began to chuckle lightly.

Tom went to the window; he wanted out. His mother, the practical one who scratched a living for them all, was a speck in the distance beyond the bog, off in the north field. He could see the flash of her spade, digging turf. His swarm of cousins, his older brother and his younger sister were doing chores. Auntie May had gone to the cattle market to sell or trade what she could.

Too ill for work, then too weak to go marketing; Tom heard his mother's voice in his head and clenched his fist in frustration. He might have gone to the fair himself, but his mother put a stop to it. Last week he'd gotten a nasty kick when he was milking one of the cows. His shoulder had ached, and he begged off chores. His mother had agreed he could rest and he and his cousin, Ellen, had sneaked out to play in the woods whenever they could. Then this morning when he was readying the wagon, his mother had hauled him by the shirt collar back into the house.

"You can sit by the fire and mend harness, black the family's boots," Noreen said. "And the windows need washing-it's the very thing to take the stiffness out of an aching joint." These days, it seemed all her high good humor had been sucked up by the endless work of the farm. Her black moods had worsened, too, he thought, since Rose moved in.

"The pot goddess made humans out of clay." The old woman shoveled a handful of soggy brown bread in her mouth and held it there a while.

His father lit a pipe. It began to rain.

At least he hadn't already washed the windows, Tom thought.

"Wash windows," Rose sang.

Was she repeating what his mother told him, or saying his own thought out loud? She stared at him with bright bird-y eyes.

"I'm going to the kitchen," Tom said.

"Right, lad." Half the day was gone, and Cedric was just fitting the nib to his pen.

Tom took the bootblack kit with him, moving toward the low door that always swung shut unless it was propped with a brick.

"Ellen's there. In the kitchen."

He turned. He was sure the old woman had said it, but she appeared to be watching the fire. His father was absorbed, absently stroking his silk vest with the flat of his hand.

"Did you say something?"

"Hmm? What?" Cecil said.

"Never mind." Tom said.

"Get on with the chores. You know better than to disturb my concentration." The pen scratched across his paper.

"Ellen," Rose whispered softly at him. Her lips were twisted in a grin; she twined the two gnarled fingers on her right hand and rocked her bony wrist back and forth, back and forth, signaling Tom.

Tom found himself watching the slow rhythmic motion as if he were hypnotized.

"You and Ellen," she breathed. "You can light fires with the mind." She tapped her temple, laughing at him soundlessly.

"Loony," he hissed back. Then he felt a faint ripple of fear and fled toward the kitchen.

He smelled potatoes, carrots and salt pork simmering in the stew pot. The big brown bowls were filled with rising bread dough. Ellen's sleeves were turned back, and she had a smudge of flour across her forehead where she'd pushed her hair out of her face with the back of her hand. Just now, Tom saw, she was spooning jam into small triangles of dough. It was one of his favorite sweets, but she didn't always have time to make it for him.

"Quince?" He put the tip of his finger into the crock.

"Currant," she said, rapping his hand lightly with the back of the spoon. "Go on with you, your mother will have my eyes if I don't get it all done," Ellen smiled.

"Let me help, then."

"Are you going to cook now," she raised one blonde brow humorously at him, but went on scraping jelly onto the dough shapes.

"I can stir—" He pointed at the cookpot.

"It doesn't want much turning."

"I'll sweep out for you—"

"And send the dust into the food," she laughed. "You sweep at the end of the day."

"Well you haven't got that much to do, or you wouldn't be making the crescent tarts. Let's go for a walk or play a game of cards." Tom pulled a chair over to the long unvarnished table where she was working and sat.

"Haven't I? Your mother left a list as long as your arm." She began pinching the edges of the pastries. "I only did these for you because I felt sorry for you. I know you wanted to go market."

"It wasn't so much," he shrugged.

"Not so much you didn't cry? Guess it was the wind I heard northering."

"Ellen—"

"I'm not meaning to make you feel bad. Honest. Don't I know we both have it hard?" Her blue eyes were very bright.

"Why don't we run away," he said dully.

"Sure we'd do fine. You twelve and me going on fifteen."

"I'd take care of you." Tom looked up to gauge her reaction. She was transferring tarts to a big oak paddle, then carrying them toward the oven, and he couldn't tell what she was thinking. "Don't you believe me?"

"Oh damn," her hands tipped sideways suddenly, and the tarts cascaded onto the hearth bricks. "Ruined. Every one."

Tom stooped to help her pick them up. "Bake them, anyway."

"They're covered with ashes—"

"Please?"

"What for?" She sounded bitter and sad. She banged the paddle back onto the table.

"Because you made them for me, and I want you to." Tom stood facing her, his fingers seemed to float up from his side, and he touched a strand of her dark blonde hair.

Ellen put her hand on his wrist, but he didn't want to let go of her, he moved his hand to her shoulder.

They were the same height, but he was thin and angular where she was already softly rounded.

Suddenly she was crying. She leaned forward, and he felt her wet face against his throat, her shoulders trembling.

"Hold me, hold me," she whispered through her tears.

His arms went around her waist.

"Kiss me," she said.

Tom looked in her eyes, hesitating.

"I want you to."

"El—" Tom stared at her lips, swallowing hard.

"Please."

Then her head darted forward, and he felt her mouth cover his. Her tongue parted his lips, and she tasted sweet. Ellen kissed his chin, his cheeks, his neck—

"We have to, we have to," she said, "so when he comes in the night I can pretend it's you."

Her mouth opened hotly onto his and he kissed her again, even as he felt the hot dagger of hatred for his father.

The rain drummed louder and louder against the windows. He'd kissed her until his mouth felt rubbed raw. Ellen wanted him to do more—she even unbuttoned the top of her sprigged dress and her naked breasts lay against the white flannel of his shirt. He was intensely aware of them, the warm fragrant smell rising off the flesh, the skin itself—a tawny golden pink. Her small palm lay over the back of his hand, moving with his as he circled and caressed. Her nipples were softer than anything Tom had ever imagined.

"You can kiss them, if you want," Ellen whispered, but he couldn't.

Tom was suddenly aware of the acrid odor of charred meat, the stew pot sputtered, bubbling wildly with a throaty sound. His hands fell away from her. "The dinner, Ellen! Quick, it's burning!"

"What of it?" Wearily, she turned her back and began to button the cotton dress.

Tom snatched the rod and swung the pothook away from the fire. "She'll hit you," he said.

"I've been hit before."

He studied her. "What's the matter? What's wrong?"

"I have something to tell you," she began.

Anxiety flashed through him, a static charge.

"I made the tarts as a farewell present..." she paused. "In a couple of months your mother'd have the priest after me, and they'd send me away anyhow. Do you know what I'm saying?"

He shook his head.

"I'm going to have a baby—"

He cut her off. "You said when he came you could pretend it was me. You just now decided to leave! I asked you to run away before, and that's what gave you the idea—the rest about the tarts is a lie!"

"Well what of it?" Ellen said. "Don't you see it's just sooner than later, when...when I'm disgraced. I can't face my mother, I have to leave."

Her voice was hard; Tom wondered if she was convincing herself. "I'll come with you," he said.

"No, stay and get what you can." She wrapped up some cheese and bread in oiled paper. She put the food in a garden basket. Ellen pawed through the cupboards, but he couldn't see what she took down from the back shelf. It was wrapped in a towel, and she slid it under the hinged lid of the basket.

He watched her lift an old brown wool cape from the peg, then slip into it.

"You mean this minute? You're leaving this minute?" Panic flooded through him. It was happening too fast.

She put one hand on his shoulder, then she ruffled his hair. "I'm glad we kissed," Ellen said. "We can remember one another by it. Always."

"Don't go." He clung to the drab cape. "Don't."

"You're sweet. I love you." She leaned forward and kissed him on the mouth. Ellen stepped away from him.

"No, you can't, you can't—"

He watched her open the back door. He saw the four lichen spotted stone steps that led up from the kitchen. The rain blew in sheets. His mother must be in the barn now, Tom thought. "You can't go. It's raining," he said.

"Be careful of Rose," she said. "Those stories about her? They're all true."

Then she was gone, hurrying up the stairs, ducking slightly as she emerged under the porch above, then bending her head against the wind and wet.

Oh Ellen, he thought, why couldn't you wait until I was older? He sat miserably in the chair by the hearth a long time after she was out of sight.

If his mother caught him in the kitchen, he'd have to admit he'd known Ellen left. When the rest of them found out she'd run away there was going to be a family uproar. His mother would rave and shout. And his cousin, the one person who could make him feel better, was gone.

He opened the rolled edge of one uncooked tart and licked the currant jelly. Wet. Soft. Sweet. Yielding. He closed his eyes and poked around the pasty with his tongue, pretending it was Ellen's mouth. He should have kissed her more. He should have done more.

Overhead, he heard the heavy thump of the front door shutting. Tom dropped the sweet and raced for the back stairs. He was almost to the parlor when he remembered the very last words she said. His chest burned with sorrow: His pig of a father had used up his pretty cousin, Rose was a hag, Ellen was gone.

2

Noreen frowned. "Well I don't know as it should be me as tells her." They didn't expect May to be back for at least a week. She ladled the stew into a plate and passed it to Cedric. Tom watched the bowl circling the long table in the dining room. It stopped in front of his grandmother.

"She's your sister, my dear," Cedric said, handing another steamy plate round.

"Not that you'd open your gob. You wouldn't say shit if you had a mouthful."

Tom's brother Bob snickered.

"Quiet and eat now. Be grateful to God you've meat on your plate," Noreen glared. "Say the blessing, Delia." His mother bowed her head, and his poor slow younger sister recited as much of the grace as she remembered.

"You're not eating Tom."

"It's burnt," he said.

"What?"

"It's burnt." He felt the eyes of the others on him. No one, not even Cedric had said a word when his mother had brought in the reeking tureen.

"Thank your slut of a cousin."

His face blanched. He pushed the plate away. "I'm not hungry."

"What about the rest of you, then, eh?" She looked at his brothers toying with bites of bread, ignoring the stew. "There won't be any waste while I'm alive, do you hear?"

Tom put his hands in his lap. No one answered her.

"You hear? Think I'm going to give it to the pigs? I won't. If you don't eat it now, it'll be on your plate for breakfast. And you'll find it at every meal until you finish it."

Cedric opened his lips very wide, as if, Tom thought, it would somehow make the taste go away, and pushed a potato in his mouth. He grimaced.

"Delicious," Rose said, laughing. Then she upended the bowl, dumping the thick stew into her lap. She tweezed a limp carrot from her dress and gobbled it.

"Rose." His mother banged her fork down.

"From the lap of the gods," Rose said. She tilted her head back and finger-fed herself a chunk of meat.

"All right, get out of here, all of you." Noreen began cleaning up the old woman with one of the frayed muslin napkins. "Delia, scrape these plates!"

His sister hesitated, fear widening her eyes.

"Just give it to the goddamned hogs," Noreen shouted.

Delia began to cry. She crumpled into a corner and flung her arms over her head.

"Oink, oink." His grandmother went on trying to eat the mess in her skirts, her hand finding its way around Noreen's fluttering napkin.

Tom felt his stomach roil. In his haste to get away, he pushed his wooden chair back so hard it fell over. He slammed the door on his mother's shouting.

It had been four days since Ellen had left. Auntie May wasn't back from the market. At supper every night his mother debated what they should tell Margaret about the disappearance. Every time Noreen brought the subject up Tom felt like he could never eat again, and Noreen got angry. "It's not burnt, it's not," she shouted.

She was making Delia do the kitchen work. His sister made cabbage soup three days running. Noreen decided May could cook when she came back. Tom could take over what chores his aunt had done. He had no illusions that it might include going to town. She made that clear.

"I'll explain it to you, how to make sure they're not cheating us, and you can go Cedric."

"Bob, perhaps—"

"Bob's needed here." His mother dipped bread into the boiled cabbage.

"It isn't that I wouldn't like to, my dear, but my manuscript is at a state—a state where I shouldn't like to leave it just now." Cedric smiled, then took a deep drink from his glass. He was the only one who had wine with dinner. The others got ale on special occasions and cider the rest of the year.

Tom saw the look in his mother's eye as she glanced at the brocade vest, the ruby color of the wine in the only goblet in the house. He realized suddenly his mother had gotten to the end of her patience. Whatever reasons she indulged Cedric all these years were coming to an end.

Noreen wiped her mouth and flung the crumpled napkin next to her plate.

"What manuscript, Cedric?"

Tom shivered at the contempt in his mother's voice, but his father didn't seem to hear it.

"Why my book, of course, darling," Cedric said. He beamed at Tom's sister. "The soup is lovely, Delia."

"There is no book, Cedric. Just a lot of used up pieces of paper and a Regency desk I scrimped and saved up for that's going to be sold to pay for the new roof on the barn."

"No."

"The man will be here Friday to pick up the desk."

"I need that desk—"

Noreen bared her teeth and shook her head, no.

"But my dear, it's all different now. There's no distraction and I've gotten on swimmingly."

"You mean the last four days." His mother laughed and reached over and seized the wine glass. "Too bad, Cedric."

"Noreen, please."

Tom heard the desperation in his father's voice.

"You tell me, Cedric, what shall I toast to?" She sipped and held the glass up, "Because the first time I caught you when that little whore came in my house, you said she'd be an inspiration. Said the writing was going like a house afire." She tilted her throat and swallowed all of the wine in a single gulp. She banged the glass down and it rang against her plate. "And now that she's gone, you're telling me you're glad to be without the distraction." Noreen's green eyes blazed. "How far are you from the end, by the way?"

"Scant pages."

"How many pages?"

"The work of a lifetime. You can't rush these things." He looked away.

"Just what I thought," she said, her lips turned down in a sneer. "All right. Get out. All of you." She stood up, and everyone scattered.

Tom saw his father leading Rose from the room, her skinny hand riding his forearm, her sunken old mouth working. She muttered something Tom couldn't catch; at the door, Cedric suddenly turned. "Noreen," he said, "I think you might be making a mistake—"

"Let me alone." Her voice was tired, her eyes had a faraway look.

Noreen stared at her pale worn hands, at the broken grimed nails and yellow calluses as if the alien hands of a stranger had been grafted onto her wrists. Then she lowered her face against them and began to cry.

In the passageway, Tom's grandmother clenched her fist into a tight knot, held it up against her shriveled lips and whispered, "It isn't sweat and tears we want, it's blood." She shook her fist.

After she hobbled into the parlor, Tom saw two small reddish splashes on the scarred wainscoting. They were wet and he rubbed them with the ball of his thumb. Blood, he thought, at the same time from behind him in the dining room, he heard his mother give out a small gasp.

"Mother," he said, reversing his footsteps and leaning into the doorway. She was wiping her hands furiously on a napkin, then pressing it hard against her palm.

"It's nothing," she said. "A blister that opened. Go away, now."

He nodded, saying nothing. But the white napkin was soaked with blood.

Tom slipped down the stairs. The fire was banked, no more than a dim red glow. His parents' argument whirled in his head. Was his father really on the verge of completing the manuscript? He felt his way in the dark to the desk. He knew there was a lamp on the right, and he turned up the wick and got it lit. The pile of manuscript pages was on the corner of the writing table. He began to glance through it. He saw it was an edited or recopied version. There were very few scratched out sentences; here and there a word was inserted or deleted with a thin black line. The stack was quite high.

He sat in the chair and opened the drawer. It was stuffed with earlier versions of his father's book. These were the pages that were smudged, crossed through, and occasionally torn where his father had saved a few paragraphs. This put a new light on his father's work. The family opinion was that Cedric spent his days smoking and scratching his chin with the tip of his pen. But here was work, honest effort. He pulled the stack of pages closer: Chapter 8, Chapter 14. Somewhere toward the middle, Cedric had neatly lettered Part IV. There were hundreds of pages of copperplate script. He skipped ahead, stacking the manuscript face down on the left. In his hands he held the last fifteen pages Cedric had written. He only scanned, but the book was exactly what he expected; his father was a devout admirer of Dickens, (had even written a letter to him but never received a reply) and the plot involved a character named Sedgewick. The pages Tom held were entitled, *In which Sedgewick Finds his Past*—clearly a conclusion. There were lots of names; threads, he supposed, his father had carried though to the end. He read some scattered paragraphs and laid all but the last few pages aside. Sedgewick was in a graveyard digging up his mother's coffin, when suddenly the pen tailed off leaving a long ragged black stroke that ran down the blank space of the white page. He squinted to read the small uneven script, cramped against the edge of the paper.

Her cunt is hot, I fill her belly to fill myself.

Cunt. His face burned. Here was a word written he'd only even heard aloud once or twice in his life. He felt his stomach muscles knot. He must've read it wrong. Wherever the thought came from, surely it wasn't on the paper. He squinted and then opened his eyes to look again.

It was there.

He moved the page aside, and looked at the one beneath it. The creamy paper was badly wrinkled, as if it'd been crushed into a ball, then smoothed it out. In the middle of all that space was the single word Ellen written three times. Just like that, *EllenEllenEllen*. It looked pale against a spattering of black ink drops, brownish smears.

Tom felt his heart beat faster. He moaned softly. His cousin's name was written in blood.

He was afraid, but he made himself look at the rest.

The pen stroked down wildly again, and on the next page he saw Sedgewick was back in gear, pulling at chunks of turf with his hands, then cutting a wider swath with a spade, his shovel at the ready to dig down.

It was like Cedric suffered a mental lapse, some kind of peculiar blank filled with dark imaginings.

He shoved the pages out of the way and put his head down on his arms. The words his father had written were terrible. He thought of Ellen crying in the kitchen, then running out to the rain, and Tom was aware inside himself there was a hollow place so vast, so empty it might never be filled again.

He'd known it, of course. He'd known, he realized, even before Ellen told him. What else had those night noises been? The creaking bedroom door, the lanternlightlantern light clicking as it moved down the hall, down the stairs. The soft half-grunts from the direction of the kitchen.

It was his father swiving Ellen. It was his father making her sleep in the room off the kitchen and creeping down the stairs at night when the rest of the house was asleep; but those small sounds had penetrated Tom's dreams. And the last noise, Tom mourned, the last noise was most terrible of all: a little girl weeping.

He blew out the light, but he didn't have the energy to climb the stairs to his sleeping loft. He sat, knees splayed in the chair, his fingertips still tingling from the touch of that page, from the awfulness of what he read. Tom shut his eyes. What in the name of Christ did sex have to do with writing?

Because as near as he could figure it, that's what his father seemed to think—that potency created a kind of magic that fed his work. Ellen was gone, and the work stopped. He rubbed his eyebrow with his fingers. There were a lot of things grown-ups said or did that made no sense, but he couldn't even begin to get any sort of handle on this one—

There was a low bubbling sound in the corner of the room. Tom sat forward. He waited. Perhaps it was just an ember sliding through the grate. There was a squeak—so low he wasn't sure he'd actually heard it. Tom stood up, trying to see across the shadowy space of the room.

He heard the soft rubbing squeak again, and he knew his grandmother was in the room. She chuckled, but the sound was like a bitter whisper.

"Not sex, no. It was the baby." The rocking chair moved more slowly than he would have thought possible. "You come here, boy." She swiveled around and pulled the drape cord. The night sky was cloudy, the moon barely visible.

He walked toward her, and he could see her rheumy eyes, the shape of her face.

She reached out and pinched the flesh of his arm. "It's dead now—that's why the work stopped." She nodded. "It's dead because she's dead."

He stepped back, and she gave him a dreadful smile.

"In a ditch, boy. She's lying there—"

"No—"

"You'll see. When they bring 'er back," she said. "You think I'm crazy don't you?" Rose laughed. "But mind, see if I'm right. He'll have to get another woman. Noreen won't give 'im anymore." She pointed toward the desk, and Tom saw her skinny arm quiver. "You're in that book—just like your brothers and Delia. But he needs another woman to finish it. Another life." Her dark eyes gleamed. "That's why I'm here, to help."

Tom wanted to run, but he stood there, afraid her hands would fall on him the second he turned.

"You're going to see," she hissed. "And you're going to help, too. You interfered, and it killed her."

Her hand snaked out and caught his shirtfront. She dragged him forward until he was wedged against the arm of the rocker. He felt the wood pressing on his thighs, and he caught a whiff of her scent. She smelled so old. He tried to turn away, but her fingers crawled higher, and she gripped his neck and pulled his face to hers.

"Your touch killed her. I set my finger on that life, and when she ran off, I had to kill her. She was going to kill herself," Rose spat viciously. "Don't you know if she killed herself your father would never have finished?" She turned on him. "She wouldn't have left if you hadn't interfered, hadn't kissed with her.

"You killed the life that fed the work of a lifetime. My boy would've done me proud. But you stopped it." Her voice went hard, and he felt her sharp nails digging in the skin of his neck. "Do it again, and see what happens."

He felt a sudden stabbing pain in both eyes. He tried to pull away, but she held onto him. He felt his skin break out in a sweat. The pain moved a notch higher and he moaned softly. Mother Mary, it's like spikes being pounded in.

He blinked, but he couldn't see. There was nothing but darkness. His hands flew up, he was sure his shaking fingers would find gaping holes. But in his panic, he couldn't tell. He would've sworn there was blood running down his cheeks. His breath came out in hot choked gasps.

She squeezed his throat, his hands tore at her wrists, and then the pain stopped abruptly, his vision cleared. "You interfere again and I'll blind you—and that'll be just the beginning of what I do," Rose said. He felt a sharp pain in his groin, he gasped, and she shook him off. Tom stumbled and landed on his hands and knees. His face was damp with tears. "Answer the door," she said.

A second later, there was the sound of rushing horses and a heavy wagon skidding to a stop. Tom heard the crump crump of footsteps hurrying along the path. Someone shouted and pounded at the wooden door of the house.

A farmer with a heavy mustache stood on the step. He stared deeply into Tom's eyes, then dropped his gaze. He held his dirty hat in both of his big hands. "Where's yer folks, lad?"

"Asleep." Tom hung on the brass knob. The man had an anxious look about him.

"Might you have a sister, now?"

"What is it? Who's there?" Noreen's voice drifted down. Tom heard his father stirring above him. Cedric's door opened in the hall.

The man spoke more quickly. "Name of Ellen?"

"My cousin." Tom felt the words bubble up on his lips.

The man wiped his eyes with his dirty sleeve. "I didn't see her, she ran in front," he pointed to the horses. "She—I didn't hit her, she jumped to get out of the way and fell over the side of a low stone bridge." He suddenly took Tom's shoulders in his hands. "Pink cloud. This here's Pink Cloud, right?" The man nodded, as if he were answering his own question. "The name were written in a little book she carried. Ellen Wood of Pink Cloud, County Meath. I drove all night."

His parents were rushing down the stairs.

"I can't tell 'em lad. She's in the cart," he whispered, backing down the steps and moving away from the house. "Her neck's broken."

So, Tom told Cedric and Noreen that Ellen was dead.

It was raining the day they were burying Ellen. Tom walked along slowly behind the pallbearers, their shoulder muscles shifting under the black woolen jackets, her wooden casket swaying. Just a light steady drizzle, he kept thinking—nothing so dramatic as the huge pelting drops she'd run out into only the week before.

Now that Ellen was on her way to the cemetery, Tom found he hated his aunt. His hatred had come to him quite suddenly. It was because May sat guard over Ellen's coffin the whole three days. She ate whatever anyone brought to her; she snatched her sleep in fits and starts; nod off, then shake her head like an old dog and begin moaning again.

It was a stupid reason to be angry, but there it was; he hated Auntie May because he wanted to say goodbye to Ellen in his own way, but he couldn't—not with her mother right in the room.

The first night, after the farmer brought her in, Tom lay awake tossing in his bed until dawn. His arms were crooked under his head, and he tried to think of what would please Ellen. Earlier, while they were laying her body on the sofa, he rummaged in the wagon and found the little red leather book the farmer told him about; it was blank beyond her name. Tom recognized it, it belonged to Cedric. He wondered when his cousin took it from the desk.

Maybe Ellen was going to keep a diary, think of the book as her friend and confidante—as Tom himself had been.

Did you ever have a nickname, he asked her once.

Never had time for one, I guess, she said, her hand plunged deep inside the sock she was darning.

They both laughed, and then she laid the sock aside, settling it on her knee and touched his hand very lightly.

Tom, she said, her eyes dark sapphires in the firelight, I don't' think anyone had enough time for me to bother about it. He looked at her questioningly and she went on. I mean, I don't think anyone ever liked me that much.

I do, he said. I like you that much—and more. He jiggled her fingers in his. C'mon then—what about Nell, or Nellie?

Ugh! Makes me sound like a fat old washwoman, she giggled.

Ellie? would you like me to call you Ellie sometimes?

Ellie, she nodded, squeezing his hand hard. We have a secret, now, she said—just like real lovers. Tom saw the color high on her cheekbones, her eyes glinting with tears.

He remembered the last day, the way her blue eyes shone, the way her voice made him tremble inside. Then sitting cross-legged on his narrow bed, Tom wrote the same words she'd spoken in the kitchen as tribute for her.

You're sweet. I love you.

Hesitating, he nibbled the tip of the pen, then added,

I have your secret now—just like a real lover.

He looked down at the flyleaf and frowned. Somehow, there ought to be more. A man, he told himself, would write more. But what more? Hard as he tried, he couldn't think what else Ellen might want to have written in her book. Maybe, sometimes it's all right to say or do the simple thing, he thought. It was an odd grown up kind of notion, but it seemed right.

He closed the book. The ink had smudged, but he was sure Ellen wouldn't mind. She wasn't a one for scolding over trifles.

He lay back, his mind churning until he was content with his plan to memorialize her. He meant to sit by Ellen's side, hold her hand and watch her sleep. When the two of them— he and Ellen—were alone, he would slip the red book in the pocket of her dress. He wanted to lean over her still form, stroke her baby yellow hair, and kiss her lips once, lightly, before they sealed the lid.

An innocent goodbye, a last farewell—but they couldn't even have that—all because Margaret made a show of her grief.

Now standing by the gravesite, listening to the useless words of the somber priest, his throat felt tight, his mouth filled with a sour taste. He watched three black rooks sitting on a tree limb, preening themselves.

The first shovelful of wet heavy dirt struck the coffin with a thump. The sound was so final, he thought; no, he amended inwardly, if you thought about it, it was no more final than the farmer's knock at the door. Both sounds heralded death.

Goodbye Ellie, he whispered into the wind. I love you. He felt the release of tears.

He looked up. Rose's mouth was working, her eyes greedily following the sexton's progress as if she herself was being filled instead of Ellen's grave. His mother's face was dark with a strange grim satisfaction. She shuffled her handkerchief from hand to hand, anxious, he guessed, to get back to her work. His Aunt May buried her face against Cedric's shoulder and cried a long wailing note.

Ellen was gone and he was left with all that hate. The thin red leather diary was still inside his shirt front, pressing heavily—an unbearable weight—against his chest.

3

"She's rotting, boy, don't you think?" Rose Smith sat by the fire, her feet in a bucket of hot water, her knobby arms and chest wrapped in a heavy shawl.

Tom didn't answer the old woman, he gave the smoldering peat a sharp stab with the iron poker. The turf tumbled downward and began to smoke; it would certainly go out, if he let it be, he hoped it would.

Since Ellen died the year before, his grandmother was thriving. She was stronger, less prone to maundering. She made sense when she talked—at least around him. The rest of the family still thought she was dotty, but Rose was as lucid as the clearest stream when she spoke to Tom. He sighed—that was part of the problem—she spoke to him often, everyday.

Somehow taking care of her turned into his job. He tried to fob it off on Delia, but his mother put an immediate stop to it. No, Delia was going to help Margaret in the kitchen, be a kind of cook's apprentice. He maintained Winston, the youngest—now five—could look after a woman in a chair, bring her tea, fetch and carry. Winston, his mother declared was going to be in charge of the hens. Everyone else was older and stronger and needed for the heavy work in the fields.

"Must be tight, lying there all day, day in and day out, the wood pressing down on your face." Rose turned bright malicious eyes on him. "Ever think about it?"

"Think about what?" Tom opened a small closet to the left of the mantel and shook out a cloth. He began polishing the low brass fender. She might fall asleep if he moved quietly.

"Death, you ninny."

He didn't look up from where he stooped, but he heard the water slosh in the bucket. "Get me a towel," Rose said. He handed her a clean rag from the closet. She grunted.

"Good enough for me, eh?" She began drying her feet.

He shrugged.

Rose laughed. "Think it rains in on 'er? Cedric was never much of a carpenter. Yer brothers are no better, nor May's boys."

"Her name is Ellen."

"You mean was." Rose scuffled to the rocker and eased herself down. "Sure," she began swaying in the chair, "it's probably a regular Brighton beach in there, tides comin' and goin'. Bet she gets flooded regular like."

Tom tried not to listen, but the image of Ellen laying in her grave with water rising made him ill. He clenched his fist. He had to say something. "Ellen's dead. She can't feel—"

"How do you know?"

Tom averted his eyes. The old hag was right, of course, how did he know? Maybe Ellen was suffering in the cramped cold space. He hated to think she was suffering.

"Course you see her in your mind's eye," she tapped her temple, "tucked in like she was sleeping—"

It was true, he hadn't let himself think of the changes—

"Not the way, she is: eyes sunken in, lank hair spouting from the skull. There's not much to her," Rose said. "The flesh running off, the bones rising through."

"Stop," he whispered.

Rose leaned forward in the rocking chair. "Cedric's still hangin' on to his idiot dreams of being a gentleman farmer an' breeding race horses; but I told 'im he's only fit for one thing—writing." She nodded sharply, and Tom saw the loose flesh on her throat quiver. "Maybe if you help me, I'll help you," she said.

He looked at her, puzzled for a second. It hit him all at once. The night noises had begun again.

"Your Aunt Margaret," Rose said. "Not the best choice, to be sure, but the only available one."

Her hands gripped the arms of the rocker. Tom saw the lawn and sky behind her through the window. He stood by the mantel, and toyed with a lacquered box his father had given Noreen for Christmas.

"You haven't forgotten our little talk that night?"

He swallowed. "Mother burned the manuscript."

Rose chuckled. "Did she? What's paper? It's words that matter."

He thought of Cedric's vagueness. "He'd never remember all."

"Maybe, maybe not," she shrugged. "But a book is a thing with a life of its own. It grows in secret." She grinned at him. "Go upstairs and see. It's all there; some's under the mattress, some's in the closet, some's tucked behind the eaves."

He hesitated, on the verge of going. "The desk is gone. And when does he write? I've never seen him, since—" he looked down, unable to say it, afraid he might see Ellen weeping on his shoulder in the kitchen.

"When do you dream?"

He was tired of her questions, confused. "What difference does it make?"

Rose began to laugh. "What difference does it make? Oh, you really are a fool." She sat forward. "We're all in that book; unless he finishes it, we'll be gone forever."

"That doesn't make sense."

"No?" She fixed her dark eyes on him. "You just mull on this: as soon as the last person dies who remembers you, you die again." She whispered, "I'm old, but I don't want to die. Help me, and I'll help you." She looked out the window, toward the burying ground, and when she turned toward him again, Tom saw she was smiling. "I'll bring her back. You'd like that wouldn't you?"

He shook his head. Things had gotten out of control. He closed his eyes and a low whine came out of his throat.

"You would like it. I know."

Tom opened his eyes and saw Rose perched on the edge of the chair like some ravening bird. Her eyes glittered, her face was shrunken, her hair wild.

"Ellen," he said her name. No sound came out of his lips.

"You can swiv her this time," Rose hissed.

Tom knocked the lacquered box to the floor and ran out the front door.

"Why doesn't he finish? You said it was all there. Why doesn't he finish it?" He was sick of hearing her talk about Cedric's book.

It was summer now, and Rose clamored for fresh air. She was in the short padded chair with wheels that Bob made for her. Tom pushed it across the lawn. She could shuffle after a fashion and get around the house, but more and more she made Tom steer the chair. The chair was a botched thing, uneven and difficult to maneuver. After a rain, the wheels left ruts in the thick grass. He often thought about dumping it over, but he was afraid to try.

She badgered him almost every day, and she crept into his dreams at night and he saw her wrinkled sneering face and heard her cracked voice taunting him even in his sleep.

He begged Noreen to let him off. He offered to do anything, he threatened to run away, but Noreen's mind was made up: Tom would look after his grandmother.

He wanted to scream in his mother's face, she's a witch! But something in his mother's eyes stopped him. He began to think Noreen kept him at the task for that very reason, that she wanted Tom to keep Rose in check somehow.

"He hasn't finished because she's not with child," Rose said. He knew she meant Aunt May.

Cedric had bought Rose a set of false teeth, and she clicked them. The sound made him grimace.

"You hear them, boy, don't you? Cedric and Margaret straining in the night?" she laughed.

He struggled with the chair up a slight incline. He dug in and pushed. Rose wanted to go to the top of the rise.

"Noreen doesn't hear them, but you do." She clicked her teeth again. "Does it make your little twig tremble?" she asked. "Does it make you think of her?"

"Shut up." Tom stood still.

"Noreen doesn't want to hear them, but you do, eh?" Her grizzled brows arched upward.

"My mother knows what you are." Tom crossed his arms.

"Not like you, though, eh?" she said.

Rose licked her finger and wet her lips, rubbing them in a slow circle, her eyes fixed on him.

Tom moaned. He felt the old woman's finger tracings on his own lips. She was working some peculiar spell. It was like kissing Ellen all over again. He would have sworn Ellen stood that close, her soft lips touching his. He felt her tongue. He smelled clean hair, closed his eyes. He felt himself stiffen and turned away, humiliated. Oh Lord, what if he—the sensation stopped.

"Help me, and you can have her again. See there." She pointed to the west. "There's a church. Outside the door is a kind of crude carving, a sheila na gig. You get it and bring it here. Know what it is?"

"No, and I don't care."

She giggled, and Tom saw her hands twitch down to her lap. He suddenly felt slim delicate fingers probe gently near the buttons of his trousers. He groaned. He was in the grip of a vision so powerful he lost track of whether his eyes were opened or closed. Oh God, the smell of her warm, clean skin. He felt himself falling, and then he was lying on the damp grass on his back drowning with Ellen.

Her blouse was spread out on the turf where she'd tossed it. Ellen straddled him. Her small breasts plumped against his chest. Her fingers moved like butterflies and nudged his shirt up. Her flesh touched his. She experimented with her tongue and teeth and nipped one of his small flat breasts. She rubbed her chin against his.

"So smooth," she murmured. She sat up and unfastened the waist of her skirt. She drew it upwards, skimming it over her arms, shoulders, head.

She had nothing on underneath, and the sight of her, the feel of her firm thighs clamping his thin chest made him nearly lose control. He bit his lip.

"Slow, my sweet." She touched one finger to his lips.

Tom fumbled, and tried to push his trousers down. Ellen moved aside and helped. The sound of the sliding cloth was maddening. She touched the light ginger froth of hair on his legs. He shivered at the sensation.

"Ah, my love." She kissed his knee. He saw her eyes focus on the pale reddish thatch in his groin. He shut his eyes, the sun burned through his lids. He felt her hair dangle against his loins. Oh God, oh God.

His lids fluttered, and he saw her lips move toward him in a perfect O.

"Ellen, no."

She giggled and stuck her tongue out, laughing. He felt her crawl forward gently and then she was on him, hips moving in a way he would never have believed possible. She arched her back, and he saw the joy on her face and he was inside her, briefly, too briefly, and it was over.

She stretched her legs and lay on his chest, her yellow hair spreading in a flood over his chin and throat. He stroked her narrow back, his hand found the wider curves below it. She smiled and he squeezed her tightly. He kissed her mouth and she sighed.

He and Ellen—his Ellie—had shared love at last.

He opened his eyes. Rose sat in her chair, laughing quietly. He sat up. He would never have believed there could be so much grief. Such sorrow. He felt like something terrible had been taken from him. Ellen was there, not there. It was more than he could bear. He looked down. A wet stain was spread across his trouser front.

"There's more. I can make it real. You can have her."

Anger and shame welled up in him. Who was she to think she could violate him this way? How dare she? It was too much, the pain, the sweetness, the grief.

He lost control of himself, his vision misted, he didn't know what he thought anymore, didn't know what was happening. There was only the blood red cloud of anger that burst inside him.

"You goddamn cunt bitch," Tom said, advancing on the old woman, his legs moving swiftly with the purpose of the stalk. His hands found her throat, and he squeezed hard.

He was going to kill her. He was going to keep sinking his fingers into her thin flesh until her eyes bulged and her tongue shot out of her mouth, and then when she was dead, he was going to rip her stinking filthy head from her shoulders.

He heard her moan and hiss.

There was nothing he could do that would be bad enough. Nothing that could make her suffer enough. Nothing.

She flopped and struggled in his grasp, her arms and legs splayed out and thumped against the chair.

"Haaahhhhh."

He heard the choking whine pour of her. He pressed harder, and the chair went over and spilled them both. He held on, grunting, squeezing.

There was a sound of running feet. Someone shouted, and he heard a crack. He felt a sharp stinging pain. Another.

A pang of regret flashed through his mind: Oh, not fast enough.

A third crackle followed by pain.

He tumbled off the old woman and lay in the grass. His shoulder throbbed, his arm felt like it was on fire. He knew the trickling sensation was blood.

Cedric stood over him, and Tom looked up at the same time his father cocked the gun again.

He heard the old hag cough. Sure, I wasn't fast enough, he thought, she's still alive. He felt his father's boot nudge his side. Then he lost himself again.

4

"Why'd you want to shoot yourself, huh, Tom?" Delia leaned over the bed. She was eating toffee, and Tom smelled the sticky sweet. His lids fluttered, and he closed them again. She had a tan ring around her mouth, where she'd licked her lips. She chewed, swallowed. He felt her poke the corners of his eyelids.

They'd told the girl he'd shot himself, he thought.

"I know you're awake. Open up." She tugged his hair. "How come you did it?" she asked, popping another piece of candy in her mouth.

"I didn't," he said. He was in his own bed, the ceiling seemed too close.

"Did it hurt?" Her jaws made a soft creak as she chewed.

"Yes." His shoulder felt like it was packed with ten pounds of dressing.

"Why'd you keep doing it then, huh?"

He smiled. "Never mind. Got any more candy?"

"No." She showed him the gooey piece in her mouth. "Bob gave me a half-sack all for myself. I ate it. It only took one morning, too," Delia said.

"It seems quiet. Where is everyone?"

"Up at the graveyard."

She must have died after all. He shuddered, and his injured arm throbbed when he flinched. He forced himself onto his side and looked into her eyes. "Gran?" He let the word hang in the air, held his breath.

"Uh-uh," Delia said. "Mother fell in a quick marsh. They stuck long poles all through it, they knew where because Papa found her shoe caught in the muck near the edge, but they can't find her. There's nothing to bury. They're just going to have the stone."

"Why aren't you crying?" He looked at this small, odd girl who was his baby sister.

She shrugged, saying, "No one is. You're not either." She pointed at him.

"It's the shock. I will though, later," Tom said. He knew it was the truth. "Why aren't you at the funeral?"

"They told me to stay here. Want some water? I'm supposed to nurse you."

"No thanks." He closed his eyes.

"Know what, Tom? Papa says I can have her room. Mother's room. I'm going to have all that room and the bed for myself."

He looked at Delia for the first time in a long while. She'd always been a little slow, and maybe that was why he thought of her as a child. But now he saw her face had lost the round baby look. She was taller. He couldn't tell under the long apron, but maybe she was developing breasts. He swallowed. Oh, Christ, not his sister. No. They wouldn't. Noreen was dead, there was no child from May. They would. Oh Jesus, Jesus. He moaned.

"Are you in pain, Tom?" Her eyes were round and serious.

"Yes." He closed his eyes and he wept.

202

He stood at the edge of the bog. His arm was in a black sling. It ached on damp days, which was nearly always, but it was healing.

Tom squatted, looking through the torn and matted grass. He was looking for something that might show there'd been a struggle. A man's heel dug in that little bit too deeply; something fallen—a fingernail paring. But there was nothing.

Was it an accident or suicide? Noreen wasn't the type to despair; that left the way clear for accident. But she wasn't the sort to wander distracted either. How had she fallen in? He'd never know. He stood up, using his good arm to help keep balance. His eye found the horizon beyond the green hills dotted with his mother's sheep. He'd never know for sure, but he guessed Rose set her finger on Noreen's life.

Cedric never said a word about the shooting or Tom's throttling of the old woman. Rose wrapped her neck in flannel and talked in a pain-blurred voice, but her dark brown eyes were as bright as ever.

He began to walk toward the hillside. He climbed the stile, carefully, and sat finally in a patch of clover, cradling the wounded arm on his lap.

The bullets had passed through, even the one that hit the bone had veered and gone out. The others had only torn muscle and flesh.

He'd gone to the rise and dug out the slugs. They seemed important somehow, not just because his father had done it, but because they made a change in him. Or maybe, they signified the change that had come just before: the vision of Ellen, the killing hate inside him. He took them from his pocket now, and tossed them lightly in his palm, catching them.

Three bullets, three lives, a voice spoke up in his mind. Ellen, his mother—he stopped. Ellen counted for two, he supposed, but no, that wasn't it. Did he mean his grandmother? Cedric? Aunt Margaret? Delia, dear sweet backward girl? Tom had called her "bunny" when she was a baby—it was how she seemed, helpless and soft.

He closed his fist around the lead balls.

He would kill Cedric if he touched the child.

Yes, I will, I will kill him if he touches Delia. Tom woke with his fist clenched, his fingernails embedded in his palms and those words spinning through his mind, uncertain if he'd actually said them out loud. He sat up warily.

Jack Cahill was lying on his side, one elbow crooked, his hand supporting his shaggy head. "Do you suppose there's a son anywhere in the world who hasn't wanted to kill his Dad?" He grinned.

Tom felt his face go red. "I talked in my sleep?"

"Heaps," Jack turned on his back. "Some was slurry o' course, but the main thrust, I gather was a dream about sweet little Eleanor."

"Ellen."

"Girlfriend?" Jack sat forward, staring at him.

"My cousin," Tom said.

"Tssk, tssk," Jack clicked his tongue. "Want to talk about it?"

"No."

"Sure you do," Jack said, uncorking his gin bottle. "You talk about it, you'll quit living it every night." He polished the mouth of the bottle with his palm, swigged, wiped it again and offered it to Tom. "C'mon, it'll help the time pass."

Tom hesitated, then reached for the bottle.

"Gin," Jack sighed. "It's more than a breakfast drink."

Tom laughed, spluttering drops of liquid over both of them.

"Don't go wasting good booze, laddie. Drink up and tell your tale."

"What's the story of your life, Jack?"

"Mine? Christ, the facts—the interesting ones, anyhow-wouldn't amount to a fart in a thimble."

Tom snorted, laughing again; he found the image deliciously funny. "No really," Tom said.

"I'd rather hear a good tale than tell one—" He put his hand up to stop Tom's protest. "But I'll tell it, later. There's a promise." His eyes met Tom's. "What's the dirt on your Granny Rose."

"She's a witch—"

"That's the ticket, keep spinnin' er out, laddie, I'm all ears." Jack lay back happily, one hand holding the bottle upright on his chest. "You take your time," he said.

And Tom told him.

He was in the kitchen, standing over Ellen's long, wooden table kneading bread when he had the feeling something like a shadow moved past the window behind him.

Tom swiveled. He heard a sliding footstep on the outside stairs, then saw Rose's leering white face framed in the diamond-paned lead window in the kitchen door.

He jumped as if he'd been stung, took three long running steps, and he was at the door. The blessed key was in the plate. Tom fumbled with it, then clicked it home.

Rose rattled the knob, and he saw her laughing.

Seconds later there was a sharp zzzing like the high whine of a saw on metal, the hot smell of ozone, and the door swung wide. Rose stepped over the threshold and stood on the broad planks of the kitchen floor.

"Thought you were done with me, eh, boy?" She grinned. Her white hair was a mare's nest of whorls and spikes that made her bony face seem smaller.

He didn't answer, he just lowered his eyes.

"May's not going to give yer dad a bairn. She's past it. Know what that means?"

"No. Only the nonsense you spout." He slung the dough into a bowl.

"If you'd get the sheila na gig, it'd be different. It's a powerful charm, boy."

"Get it yourself."

"I can't. It's buried."

"Can't? Why don't you witch it out of the ground?" Tom said. "I'll stay right here. Go ahead, call it up. Bring it right to the kitchen door." He slapped the table hard with the flat of his hand. "Put it right here."

"It wants a man to dig it out, it needs a sorceress to make it work," she said slowly. "A child is made by both." She stared at him, and he felt the power of her gaze. It was as if, with an invisible finger, she tilted his face up to look in hers.

"Hag," he muttered.

She snickered softly, and again he felt the tug of the unseen hand pulling him.

"A hag is a holy woman, a priestess. Yes, I'm a hag. But you're like the others with your puling breast-beating faith. Precious Brigit, the nun, the saint! She was Brigantia, a goddess!"

She stood straighter, and Tom saw a change come into the old woman, as if something shone through her, animated her. Was it belief? She had the look of someone...he moaned. Mary, mother of God, she looked like Ellen, an older more matronly Ellen—but her stance, her eyes, her voice belonged to his sweet cousin.

"Brigantia was three in one, she was the fount of the poets, her sisters were the patrons of healing and smithcraft,"

Rose said. She clasped her hands together, a look of ecstasy spread across her face. "Is she not worthy of your worship? Her shrine was at Kildare, her votaries were kelles—sacred harlots. In India she was Kali Ma, the bringer of life and death." Rose paused. "She made humans out of clay." Her voice went high with excitement. "Do you know what the sheila na gig is? The goddess revealing the mystery: the way into death is also the passage of life. Souls do not die, they pass into the bodies of the living, so said the old Celtic mothers, and so it is."

She sagged all at once. Her shoulders drooped, her breathing was heavy. "My soul will not die, but it's weary, boy, and it needs a place to rest." The eyes that peered at him were old, sharp with wariness, hooded with thick wrinkled lids.

Then as Tom watched, she seemed to grow paler and paler...and finally, fade. He would have sworn he saw her dragging up the stairs—he swallowed—it wasn't so: Rose had disappeared as easily as any ghost.

It was all gibberish. It was senility and maundering dressed up as myth, he told himself later that night. She's really gone round the bend at last, and I'd be as balmy as her to give any of it thinking room. He chewed one nail, wincing when he bit too deeply along the quick. He saw a thin line of blood well up and wiped his fingers on his pants.

He knew he ought to go up to bed; instead, he blew out the lantern in the kitchen and climbed the outer staircase. It was cloudy, there were no stars, no moon.

Tom walked to the top of the rise: if he strained he could make out the steeple of the old church. He felt safe just looking at it. Inside were the images of the saints, the Virgin, the Christ himself. The Church was a haven, a cradle for its dear babes swinging gently through life and into death.

Sure, we'll be burying Granny Rose soon, and I'll be the first to light a candle for her demented soul. He pictured the old woman lying in her coffin, a heavy silver rosary wound through her knobbly fingers. Dead is dead, boy, he told himself, and when she's gone, you'll be free of her. Let the devil listen to her trash and noise. He leaned against the broad trunk of a beech tree.

He saw the cross at the top of the church. Of course he knew the cemetery was alongside, and he knew the tales. He picked up a fallen stick, idly peeling the bark from it.

He caught the flash of a small blue light flickering in the churchyard. Tom chuckled at himself. Here were the heebie jeebies and old stories come to life. You're making yourself see it. And what do you think it is, the dead walking? He watched the light swing up and down, back and forth, tracing and retracing the same pattern.

He flung the stick aside and began to walk down the slope toward the dark misty light. But when he reached the bottom, he was surprised to find himself there. How long had he been standing here? He turned briefly and looked back at the huge beech on the rise. Just ahead he could see the door of the church, the low iron fence, the vague whitish shapes of the headstones.

He paused. There's nothing there, there's no such thing as a sheila na gig part of him argued.

Will it hurt then, to look? A voice spoke up in his mind. Just to prove it finally?

He moved quickly, barely aware of his own footsteps. He forced himself to look away when he scuttled past Ellen's grave, and he didn't stop until he stood in front of the wooden church door, his eyes roving to the heavy rounded stones of the walls. Such a lot of work to build a church. A labor of love. Think of it, hauling the boulders, dressing them, mixing the mortar, building it higher and higher—all to make a shrine of worship.

He sat on the lowest step, and leaned against the one above. The grass under his feet was thinner than it was a few yards off, because, he told himself, lots of people went into the church. They went to pray because they believed—

No, because they feared. The church was made by men, and men feared the power of the goddess.

He winced, straining to look through the trees, the deep band of shadows; but the voice that seemed to be everywhere and nowhere went on.

You're not afraid, though, are you? Get it, find her—she wants you to.

The voice was so neutral, so utterly persuasive. It might have been Rose, it might have been Ellen. Was it Ellen calling him? He looked toward the graveyard, dimly aware the tendons in his neck were creaking. But there was nothing— not even the foggy blue lights that lured him down from his place on the rise.

The wind blew gently, and he felt it dance against his cheek, ruffle his hair. He sat forward, elbows on his knees, chin cupped on his right palm. The wind rose a little higher and he could hear a soft song underneath the rustling trees.

The old woman's voice got caught in his head like a fairy tune he couldn't shut out.

Souls don't die, they enter the bodies of the living. I can bring her back. Souls don't die—

"Bring Ellen back?" he said, suddenly aware the sound of his own voice woke him. He'd been sleepwalking—or something very like it, and now he was standing near the left corner of the church, close to the rust-eaten rail that fenced in the graveyard.

The way into death is also the passage of life.

There wasn't any gate—just a wide gap in the ironwork. Two short stone pillars anchored the fence, one of them heaved and canted by the massive roots of a tree. He passed between the pillars, his eyes scanning the slightly irregular circle of tall oaks that ringed church, cemetery, grounds—his eyes flitted from one tree to the next and the next.

A sacred place, a holy place—the voice breathed.

Tom shivered. Was this ground sacred, holy in some way that was older than the church, than any church?

His ears caught the sound of soft chanting behind him. He whirled around, seeing the ancient beech towering the top of the rise. He heard the low bleat of a winding horn. A flickering line of lights began moving down the slope. Small spots of candleflame appeared, disappeared, returned. Now he could make out shapes descending in the darkness. Hooded figures from some distant time swaying in...

...a procession to the sacred grove, the place they carried the ritual sacrifice. They nailed the body to the tree—always the same tree, always the same way: first the elbows were spiked, then the forearms and hands were pinned at right angles to the joints. They fastened the knees so they were turned out, left the legs and feet hanging down. The sacrifice was left to wait, to watch them honor their mother—

"The mother," Tom whispered, and his eyes went to the enormous oak near the opening into cemetery, the gateless stone pillars beckoning him. The opening was like a throat, he thought—

No, a passage. The way into death is the way into life. She waits for your release. She lies buried at the base of tree. The Roman priests tore her image from the doorway of the church. Only find her and the waiting will be over. Don't you feel her power?

A half dozen lurching steps brought him to the scarred trunk of the oak. He knelt, and his hands twitched at his side. He seized a clot of damp turf, clawing at the grass and dirt. What was he doing, was he going to dig with his bare hands?

Take her....

He squatted, using the muscles of his thighs and back as leverage and tugged furiously at the raw earth. He grunted, straining and yanking: a great chunk came up all at once. He saw there was a ragged depression about eight inches in diameter, maybe two or three inches deep. Beetles scurried and ran, madly burrowing deeper.

He dug with both hands, throwing fistfuls of dirt aside. His fingers scraped against a sharp rock embedded in the ground, and he cried out in sudden pain.

He sat back, breathing hard, his hands plunged into the soft scatter of fragrant soil around the hole. When the pain eased up, he worked to loosen the stone, poking his fingers around its edges, cutting more deeply around it. He pulled, feeling it give way a little, then break free.

Instantly he bore it down, wielding it like a hand held hammer stone to smash at the hard earth. He scooped out the broken soil, and now the hole was some ten inches deep.

Near the bottom he touched the tip of something root-like and humped under his fingers. He felt it carefully, a little puzzled. He brushed more dirt away; it was her, oh he knew it! He chortled and went to work with a will, digging deeper until he could put both his hands around her.

Tom gave one more hard, satisfying tug, and the carved wooden image was in his hands.

He couldn't believe what he held.

The dark face was a leering goblin, its tongue lolled obscenely. It was some kind of goddamn toad. He turned it slightly. No, not an animal; it was a naked squatting woman, knees up, hands between her scrawny legs to show off her— her—the round slick hole of her privates.

Touch it, a voice in his mind whispered.

He put his index finger into the deep cleft between the legs, and he shuddered.

Then he set the sheila na gig on the ground, and lay back, one arm thrown over his face.

He was suddenly exhausted.

211

He didn't know how long he was lying on the damp grass. The air around him seemed to grow warmer. He heard a soft sigh, smelled the rich humid odor of exotic spices.

He was pinned to the spot, unable to move, and he would've sworn on his mother's soul that a young woman with plump thighs walked toward him, breathing musk and sensuality. The hem of the gauzy veils that hung to her ankles trailed over his naked body. She stooped briefly: Her moistened fingers lingered over him, gently caressing his mouth, the side of his cheek.

Then she walked past, and she seemed no more than another of the pale marmoreal shapes among the carved white head stones and cold shadows.

He sat up, alone in the churchyard. It was almost dawn and he could see Ellen's grave, the low mound of thick grass that covered her. The turf where he dug out the ugly obscene carving was healed and whole. The sheila na gig was gone.

Tom felt a deep unsettling shift inside himself. He held out his hands expecting to see them swollen and raw with his frenzied digging, but there was nothing.

He looked up toward the enormous beech tree at the top of the rise, and he suddenly shivered, hugging himself in the cold morning air.

He got up and began to walk back to the house.

When he got there Cedric was waiting up for him, sitting in the kitchen with a mug of coffee laced with brandy. His grandmother Rose was gone. She wandered out sometime in the night, and they feared she'd been lost like poor Noreen to the thick quickmud of the bogs.

At the news, Tom felt relief wash over him like a baptismal tide.

5

"Your cousin Donald's gone to have a look round for her," Cedric said, his eyes, overbright with anxiety, his face wax pale in the shadowy kitchen. He knotted his fingers, then abruptly got up for more brandy, pouring a healthy tot into the white mug. "She'll come back, she has to help me." he said.

"Right." Tom wished Cedric would leave; his father's sighs into the brandied coffee were getting on his nerves. He began slicing bread for something to do. He was hunting up butter in the corner cupboard when he heard the thick ruffle of a deep snore. Tom turned and saw his father's head lolling on his thin shoulder, the mug of coffee dangling from his limp hand. Cedric had actually fallen asleep holding onto the handle. At the same time Tom was tip-toeing forward, intent on retrieving the cup, the sound of low snickering came to him.

Rose stood on the threshold. She opened her hands wide, like a priest begging blessing, and the mug fell to the floor with a clatter, splintering into white flecks and shards. Cedric snored on.

"You did well," she nodded at Tom.

"I did nothing." He averted his eyes, then fetched a broom. He stooped over the broken cup, beginning to sweep.

She smiled broadly, showing a mouthful of strong white teeth. "Don't you want what's rightfully yours?"

Puzzled, Tom blinked. Why had he thought it was Rose at the door? Rose was gone; hadn't Cedric said so, not ten minutes before? He blinked again and stared across the length of the room. Time seemed to stretch into something that looked like the long mouth-blown shape of an hourglass.

He looked up, and a low sigh came out of his lips.

It was Ellen.

Ellen stood in front of him. The half smile he loved was on her face. Her yellow hair was pinned up, a few curling tendrils softly fanning her throat. Her arms were full and round, her waist nipped in by a wide black belt. Her dark blue skirt hung to her ankles. She had little velvet slippers on. He saw there was a line of dark loamy earth along the soles. She must've been walking through a muddy lane.

"Ellen."

"I've missed you Tom," she said. "Tell me everything. Tell me what you've been doing? Most of all tell me you wished I'd never gone."

"Ellen, Ellen." He began to weep, then he laughed and wiped his eyes with his sleeve. "Ellen, I thought my heart—never mind. Don't mind me at all. I—"

Ellen found a perch on the wooden settle by the fire. "This is new."

He nodded. "Yes," he said. He was so overwhelmingly happy, he didn't know what to say, where to begin. He sat next to her and took her small hand.

She suddenly laughed cheerfully. "You thought I was dead didn't you?" She wagged her finger at him.

"But—" He felt confused, embarrassed.

"I saw my gravestone." She laughed again, then ruffled his hair. "Tom, honestly, you've got to promise that when I've really gone, you'll see to it I've a nice angel. That skull is horrid!"

"Noreen." He hung his head.

"I never knew she had such a morbid streak," Ellen said. "Where is Noreen?" She pulled up her skirts to her calves and stuck her feet toward the fire. The sight of her damp white stockings made him groan inwardly with desire.

"Ellen." He played with the tips of her fingers. "Where have you been?"

"Does it matter?"

"No, oh no." He kissed her, and he felt himself on the verge of some sweet dreamy mystery. He wanted to rush to take her all at once, and yet, at the same time, savor each touch, each nuance in her voice, every spark of light that beamed out from her eyes.

Her hands were in his hair. He bent his head and kissed her wrists, her arms, he felt himself going hard. He kissed one thigh through the soft blue skirt. "I want you, Ellie, this time for real," he whispered.

She suddenly seized his face between her palms, and he looked up at her.

Rose stared back with bright malicious eyes. She began laughing. She coughed, then pounded her thin bony chest, and doubled over.

He pushed out at her, and she rocked against the sidearm of the bench. It wobbled underneath their weight.

He jumped to his feet. Jesus Christ, he'd kissed that hag on the mouth—had been about to raise her skirt, lick between her thighs, make love!

215

He rubbed his lips, spit, and rubbed again. His heart was pounding. This was a thousand times worse than the insidious vision that day on the rise—he'd actually touched her, kissed her—worse, wanted her.

He began to retch and heave, but there was nothing to vomit. His guts contracted painfully, he felt the wrench of the spasm. Oh God. Oh God. Part of him wanted to die.

"The power of the goddess, boy. You see it now, don't you?"

"I don't know what you're talking about!"

"Don't you? Then look at your hands, look at mine." She held out her twisted bony fingers, then turned the palms up.

They were red; slimy, slick with blood.

He looked at his own hands and saw thick dark blood coating them.

Rose had blood on her cheeks where he'd touched her. Smears were painted along her collar and shoulder. He raised his hand to his scalp, and found more sticky blood matting his hair.

"You touched the goddess, she paid us both in blood," Rose said.

"No—"

"The way into death is the way into life, boy." She nodded. "Blood is its emblem."

Cedric suddenly sat upright in the chair, his lids quivered and he opened his eyes. "Ah, mother. Thank all the saints, you had us that worried."

She went to his side and touched his shoulder. "Sleep now, the work will go on."

Cedric nodded, and his eyes sank shut.

Rose pinched Tom's cheek, and he felt his stomach roll. "Any time you want Ellen, you've only to look for her."

"I'm going to kill you," he said.

She shook her head, laughing at him, and Tom watched her climb the narrow steps to the first floor.

Tom told himself he must never allow himself to think of Ellen again. It was his love for Ellen the old woman played on and used against him. A terrible numbness stole through his bones; he felt bleached out, weak. Vowing not think of Ellen was like losing her all over again.

Tom sank onto the hard wooden settle, and put his bloodied head in his hands. He began to cry.

Six months later the night noises started up again, and even though it bothered him, (and now that he was more aware, he often threw himself stomach down in the bed and pulled the pillow over his head and ears) at least he knew the sounds well enough to recognize Margaret's gasps and moans. He supposed the neighbors were clacking their tongues, but Cedric's own mother was in the house, so it stopped the priest from bothering them. It was laughable; the idea of Rose as a chaperone made Tom's eyes roll.

No one told him what to do anymore. No one told anyone what to do. His brothers worked half-heartedly, but without Noreen's energy behind them, more and more was left undone.

Margaret spent her days leafing through fashion plates. She wore scent and went about the house in a Chinese silk robe. She read novels and quarreled with anyone who listened.

The house seemed to Tom to be tumbling about their ears, yet Margaret bought furnishings. At first it was a pretty china candlestick or a French clock for the mantel; then she began to order more: a pianoforte, wrought iron garden benches, statues, vases, tables. The parlor was cluttered, but Margaret kept on buying. It was her announcement at supper one evening that a carriage with silk appointments was being delivered that started what turned out to be Tom's flight.

LISA MANNETTI

Cedric sat at the head of the lace-covered table. His cheeks and nose were inflamed hideous pink from drinking wine. Margaret sat on his right. She leaned over and took a morsel of cheese from his plate, chewing daintily, then smiled and stroked his hand.

Tom fumed inwardly. Couldn't she hide it, while they all sat right in the same room?

Bob opened the tureen and stirred with a ladle; a thin steam rose up. "Oh Christ, Delia, not again."

"It's my specialty," she said, smiling.

Tom watched Cedric pat his sister's hand.

"I'm sick to death of cabbage—can't you at least put a bite of meat in it."

"It has potatoes—" Delia began. Her face had a panicky look.

"M-e-a-t. Meat," Bob said. He turned to Cedric. "We can't be working all the day and come into this—"

"No meat." Delia sobbed. "Animals. It isn't right."

"There, there." Cedric soothed.

Tom felt a quiver of anxiety. Bob wasn't going to let it alone.

"Fine, fine!," Bob said, throwing both muscular arms up and out in a wide vee. "Then why the hell can't she cook?" He pointed to Margaret.

"I do!" Margaret shouted.

"I don't call bringing up a wheel of cheese and slicing bread cooking," Bob turned away from her, his eyes blazing at Cedric, "do you?"

"Well—"

"The only time we have a decent meal is when Tom cooks it," Bob said.

"Then let Tom cook!" His aunt pushed back from the table.

Cedric followed. She stood by the oak sideboard sobbing. He put his arm over her shoulder. Cedric gave her his handkerchief. "Thank you," May said. She blew her nose. Cedric whispered in her ear. She lowered her voice, but not

218

nearly enough, Tom realized. "And I had such a nice surprise planned, too. Yes, the new carriage."

"What." Bob's voice was dead level. "What did you say?"

"Your aunt has ordered a lovely vehicle—"

"Goddamn it. Look, just look at this," Bob shouted. He seized Winston by the shirt cuff and tore it. "This child is wearing rags and you're ordering enough to fill a castle. Is that what you think this is? A castle? Look around, May." Her name sounded like an obscenity in his mouth. "Look at the dust," he smeared one finger along the sideboard. "Look at the dirt and the filthy goddamn muck." He shook a yellowing curtain. "Look at you, a fat whore wearing a Chinese costume."

"Cedric," she pleaded.

"Leave him out of it—I'm talking to you, not him," Bob said. He stabbed his index finger over and over at his brawny chest, like savage punctuation marks: "I do the work, I sell the goods that pay for your junk and toys. Me. I'm the man. I—" his hand dropped to his side, he couldn't go on. He suddenly lifted one of the chairs as if he meant to throw it, but he banged it down. Bob sagged, his head drooping, his thick dark hair falling in his face. Suddenly he sniffed. He wiped his eyes with his sleeve. "O the hell with it, I'm done with the lot of ye." He left the room.

Tom knew Bob would be gone when they all woke up, and he was right.

Another year went by, Tom was nearing sixteen. They never heard from Bob, he never wrote in all that time. Gradually, his cousin Donald took over Bob's old jobs and Tom did as much as he could about the place. He found a local lad of twenty, who had a wife and a new sprat on the way. In exchange for helping out with the farm chores, the young man received a small rough cottage surrounded by three acres. Tom let him keep all the produce on the plot. Next year, he'd find another tenant farmer, he told himself; and, if the profits were better, he could buy more land.

He spirited some of Margaret's purchases out of the house on the sly and sold them. Margaret cried whenever he did it, but Cedric never said a word. Tom used the money from Margaret's furniture to send Winston to school. It wasn't the best education a person could get, but at least Winston wouldn't grow up rude.

Tom let Delia do as she pleased. Some days she played with the chickens. Some days she gathered flowers in the woods. He taught her her prayers and he saw to it that she had decent shoes, flowered dresses, hats. He let her make her specialty once a week, and if it did take all day for the girl to put a few wilted cabbages into the pot of boiling water, Tom felt her smiling pride was worth a dull dinner.

Most importantly, he stayed away from Rose. He became convinced he animated her power over him by being afraid, by thinking about her, by watching her. No more, he promised himself, and it had worked. He could be in the same room now, and not look at her, not let himself know she was even there. It was, he told himself, a matter of will.

He was in the kitchen; the door was open to let in the weak September sun, and he was scouring out a skillet, daydreaming. Cooking had unleashed a new side in him, another dream, and he planned to be a chef. He would tour Europe, train with a French master and perhaps cook for the queen herself one day. He liked to picture himself with a scullery full of underlings who did the scut work, while he strutted about the great shining kitchen, the staff waiting in silence until he tasted: "Sorry, lad, needs more marjoram." Or, to another, "This omelet wants chervil." Of course, he himself would prepare the most complicated dishes, the fancy sauces and creamy desserts.

Now, he checked the mutton roast, and began doing the vegetables. Three apple pies were cooling on the sill.

"It's my day." Delia skipped down the steps. Her cheeks were flushed.

"Tomorrow is your day." Tom saw she held a drooping bouquet of overblown yellowing tuberoses. They need water, darlin'," he said and handed her a glass pitcher.

"Oh." She looked up at him. "The flowers?"

"Put them in and fill it." He watched her go out to the pump, and went back to his work. She came in and settled at the long wooden table. He looked up to see her putting the blooms one at a time into the pitcher. "They're too tall. You'll have to pinch the bottoms, see? Then they won't lean like drunken sailors." He showed her, and she laughed.

She put her face in the flowers and sniffed deeply. "No scent left." She tilted her head back and inhaled again. "Tom are you cooking an animal?"

"It's all right, really."

She sighed. "I smell it." She stuck one of her long light brown braids in her mouth. The weaving was uneven, but Tom let her do her hair as best she could.

"Don't do that, Delia."

"I'm hungry."

"There's candy in the jar." He handed her a carrot to peel.

She scraped the crooked orange root slowly. "The peppermints, right? I don't like them. They're too red." She crunched down on the carrot meant for the pot.

"What do you mean?" He opened the door and peeked at the roast.

"Red scares me Tom."

"And why is that?" He half-smiled thinking she would take up the subject of meat again.

"I used to get red, oh, a lot," she said confidentially. "It was red, you know, in my—between things," she finished. "Blood, it was blood." She nodded.

221

He stopped, the towel frozen in the act of wiping his hands.

"But not anymore, not for—for a long time. Don't you think that's better? It doesn't hurt. And, of course, Tom, it's not messy." She started on another carrot.

He was going to cry, he knew it. Oh, Jesus, what an idiot I've been. It had happened and he hadn't even suspected Cedric. Noreen and Ellen hadn't been there to tell her, help her. He looked at her, at the faint, faint swell of her small abdomen, at the slight heaviness in her young bosom, and he thought his heart would break.

He came and took her face in both hands. She looked up at him, her face filled with astonishment. He kissed her brow.

"Tom, are you crying?"

"No darlin'," he said.

Tom doused the fire in the cookstove so the roast wouldn't burn and went up the steps to sit in the yard.

Hours later when he came inside, his mind was made up. There was nothing supernatural here, he told himself. Poor blighted Delia's condition was the result of lunacy. His father was just an insane, cruel man who liked to lord power over a defenseless child...a helpless trusting child. Margaret wasn't enough for him; no, Christ no, fifty women wouldn't be enough, because it wasn't a woman Cedric wanted, it was a girl-child. Something was broken inside him—inside his brain or his heart or his soul—and it would never be fixed.

Delia and his father. Ashamed, Tom shook his head; it was all so sordid, so awful. He didn't think he could live in the midst of such horrible madness.

He was going to poison them all, and maybe himself as well.

6

Oleander was the key. Every part of the bush was lethal: the roots, the flowers, the leaves. He would grind some of the plant into a pulp and put it into their food.

He laughed to himself; what a joke May's purchases had turned out to be. She wanted an English garden and she'd ordered two huge wooden boxes to flank the entrance, and inside the peeling green tubs were oleanders. They were drooping things, neglected as the rest of the garden, but that of course, wouldn't matter. Tom sighed. Rose first, then Cedric and Margaret—and maybe, maybe the others.

Delia often carried Rose a cup of tea, but he couldn't let the girl bring Rose the poison. It would be using Delia's innocence, and that would make Tom like Cedric. That meant he'd have to find a way himself. But Rose wasn't going to take any cup of tea from Tom's hand, that was certain. So how? He imagined himself cramming a handful of twigs and leaves between the old woman's lips and clamping his hand over her mouth and nose until she swallowed.

The viciousness of the fantasy pleased him, but it was too uncertain. She might make enough noise to draw the others, and this time Cedric might not aim his gun at one of Tom's arms. Besides, he wasn't sure how much oleander was required to kill a person, and he needed to know. He sat and thought about it: the chickens were too small to test, but a sheep or a sow would be about right.

He waited until full dark and sneaked out to the yard, hastily breaking off twigs from the center of the bush where his depredations would least likely be noticed.

Then, he crept down into the kitchen and began mashing the plant up in an old pot with a wooden spoon he planned to burn in the fire when he was done. He added water, and set it to boil. While he waited, he scrubbed his hands over and over with the strongest soap he could find.

He had a thin gruel when he was done. He was too tired to go chasing after one of the sheep, so he went to the hog pen. There was an old sow named Penny who was past breeding. She was destined to be slaughtered soon, anyway. He carried along the pot he boiled the oleander in; earlier he'd tossed in some kitchen scraps and stirred it up. Now, he held it under Penny's snout and she snuffled it up, grunting happily at this unaccustomed late night treat.

The tension sapped his energy. Tom sat wearily against the wall of the barn where he could watch her. Nothing much seemed to be happening. In a little while, the moon came up, and he dozed lightly.

When he woke up the pig was dead.

Penny's death proved how quick and fatal oleander was; the problem, Tom knew, was that his grandmother wasn't going to wolf down a poisoned dinner that no one else was eating just on his urging. The other problem was he didn't know how much—or what kind of—taste oleander leant to a dish. Was it nasty? Bitter? Cloyingly sweet?

He tried sniffing at the pot, but all he got was a vague peculiar odor—some bizarre smell that was like a bad combination of lavender and very old bay leaves. And then he had another thought. It wasn't dawn yet, no one knew the pig was dead—so why not serve up Penny herself with a dash more oleander and plenty of garlic to disguise any hints of the plant's deadly flavor?

Delia wouldn't eat it of course, but if the rest of them were dead, who would look after her? He suddenly realized his thoughts had undergone another change. He didn't really want to kill Margaret, and there was no reason at all to kill Donald, his cousin. And maybe—he felt his eye tic in a jerking spasm—maybe he himself didn't want to die just yet.

Tom finally worked it out. He would smoke the poisoned hog meat. The next time Donald was due for a trip to one of the markets, he'd put a few bills in Margaret's hand and send her off on the trip as well. He imagined the conversation. "Ssh, don't tell, it's for you. Go and buy yerself something grand." Margaret was just greedy enough to fail to stop and think it was Tom who'd been selling her furniture. Winston was at school. That would leave Rose, Cedric, Delia and himself. How could he prepare them something and be sure his own portion wasn't poisoned? He couldn't.

But if all went well, he'd leave their bodies to rot at the table, take his sister and flee. He and Delia would change their names and lose themselves in another country, another life. Tom would make sure no one ever found them.

The pork hung in the smokehouse all that autumn. Tom held his breath every time he checked on it. He was half afraid wild dogs or badgers would get at it, and a spate of small furry poisoned bodies around the farm would arouse suspicions. But the quartered animal hung unmolested. It was getting colder, the crops were in. Everyday, he expected Donald to announce he was going to market. Tom counted and recounted the folded notes he'd stuffed in an old lard crock in the kitchen. There was enough money for Margaret to buy a dozen Chinese robes if that was what she wanted.

He was so keyed up, he jumped at the least sound. Every day was a torture. He realized all kinds of nervous gestures had crept into his behavior. He raked his hands through his hair, talked to himself, bit his nails, pinched one cheek when he sat and thought. It was the strain of waiting, he told himself, the strain of planning two deaths, even if both people deserved to die.

He was so distracted it was as if he wore blinders or suddenly lived inside some dank underground tunnel. But he forced himself to look at Delia. He wondered if she knew, but it was too painful to think about; it reminded him of—of her that had been.

There wasn't much belly to see, really, he told himself, but he wasn't sure when Cedric had gotten to her. He often went to the village and lingered in the shop to hear gossip from the farmers' wives until he could reassure himself her pregnancy wasn't too far advanced. He knew sometimes women did things to stop a baby, but he couldn't find out how it was done. He was afraid to ask anyone directly, and the low talk among the women never touched on the topic.

He was no midwife. What was he—what were they— going to do when the baby came? All of it seemed terrifying.

He dreamed of Delia giving birth to monsters in a gush of black blood, himself helpless. He saw her death a hundred times and woke up with the sweat clinging to his body.

And then, what? How would they care for an infant?

He stayed in the kitchen cooking more food than anyone ate, beating up batters for cakes he gave to the pigs, his mind always torn between the images of the smoked pork and his sister's swelling abdomen.

And then, he thanked God, Donald and Margaret left one dawn. Margaret took the bills Tom pressed on her and drove the wagon, heaped high with produce. Donald looked after the sheep. Tom watched the flock moving down the road. He knew the sound of their bells, their lightly trotting hooves and throaty baying would never leave him.

He ground his teeth in anxiety and walked directly to the smokehouse.

"It's your day." He found Delia fluttering her long white apron to feed the peeping chicks.

"No, tomorrow," Delia said, returning to the bin and filling her apron with more grain.

She was right, of course. But she'd never been clear on time before. How did she know? He cleared his throat, and tried another question. "Delia, how long has it been since you saw the—ah, the blood?" He tried to sound casual. He squatted down, stretching out a hand absently for one of the stirring chicks.

"You shouldn't ask that, it's for girls."

He ignored the implications. Someone—Rose or May—had told her that; so they knew. "Yes, but how long?"

"Five months."

"Are you sure? Answer carefully, darlin'."

"Yes, yes I'm sure, Tom!"

She was annoyed, a mood he'd never seen in her before. Christ help us, he thought. All right, just get her to make the soup. "C'mon, come to the kitchen now," Tom said.

"No. It's not my day."

"So do it for me, then, I'm dying for some soup." He couldn't believe the word had slipped out.

She looked at him narrowly. "All right," she sighed. "Let me get Gigi."

He was relieved. He started toward the kitchen. When he looked back, she was following.

"I've got everything ready for you. I've even drawn the water." Tom said, standing in front of the table with four green cabbages heaped on the wooden boards. "Want to put caraway in today?" He smiled as naturally as he could, but it felt more like a grimace; his mind was focused on the oleander stew bubbling in the pot behind him.

"No," she shook her head. "Gigi hates seeds."

"Who's Gigi?"

"My baby."

He didn't know what to say. He looked at her and she pointed to a small shape wrapped in a white towel lying on one of the chairs.

"Ah, a doll."

"She's more than a doll, Tom."

"Of course, darlin'," he nodded. "Want me to help?"

"Peel the potatoes."

"You're the chef. I'm just the hired help today," Tom said. He went to the basket and selected the firmest ones he could find. He set the small paring knife against the skins.

"Tom, you haven't rinsed them."

"Ah, you caught me there." His mind was a whirl. "I'll just take them to the pump. Hand me that basin."

He went outside, unable to believe how fast his heart was beating. With each passing second, his fear grew. Now it was only hours before Rose and Cedric would be eating the poisoned meat. He and Delia would eat her soup. He pictured himself sitting at the table, shrugging, pretending he was eating it to please her. Cedric would be fooled. If only Rose would get a few mouthfuls down her goddamn gullet before she got suspicious it would work. Then, he'd get Delia out of the room, and after they were dead, away from the house.

He came back inside and turned the stew. The smell of garlic and onions made him want to retch. "Mind if I use a few of yer spuds for me own humble creation, chef?"

She laughed. "Take all you want."

"Thanks." He peeled four and put them in the pot. He turned the meat again so it wouldn't stick. He ladled a small dollop of the gravy and put his tongue out.

Delia was dropping hunks of cabbage into the big blue kettle he set out for her. "See, Gigi, it's just the way you like it."

He nearly screamed at the sound of her voice. He jumped back. Out of habit, he'd almost put the spoon in his mouth to taste. Oh, thank you Jesus, he thought. He controlled his shaking hand and laid the spoon across the heavy rim. He closed his eyes; his heart skipped, and he put his hand to his throbbing chest.

"See, honey?"

He turned. Delia was holding the white bundle over the mouth of the pot. She set it on the table, and Tom saw something dark peeking out of the cloth.

"What is that?" He started to pick it up. "You never played with dolls." The spoon suddenly fell with a small plop into the kettle. His shoulders twitched at the sound.

"Give her to me, give her to me," Delia whined.

Christ, he raked his hands through his hair, you've got to be more careful. Suppose the spoon had fallen outward onto the floor and Delia picked it up? He better just leave it in the stew.

She snatched up the doll and cradled it against her bosom. "She's mine. All mine." Delia stepped back. Her face was flushed with anger. Then she suddenly hung her head. "I'm sorry. You can look if you want."

He almost didn't. He was still panicky at the thought of nearly eating the poison, he was worrying about what would happen later. But Delia was already unwrapping the figure.

In her arms was a stylized stone carving. The thing was a woman, knees up and splayed apart, hands between her legs to show off her, her—

"Her yoni," Delia said aloud.

He stared at her, stricken. He shook her shoulders. "What? What did you say?"

"Her yoni." Delia's eyes filled with tears and they spilled in a rush down her face. "She's magic, she's making my baby grow, Tom. It's a sheila na gig."

He heard a click in his brain.

Sheila na gig.

At the words he felt himself possessed. What in the name of Christ had he been thinking about all this time? What, What, *What?* He must've been crazy, half out of his mind with grief and the plotting. And here he was, pretending that goddamn bitch didn't exist. Didn't count, because Tom Smith, protector of the young and future chef, ignored her. He shook his head. What a fool you are. His head moved back and forth in a slow arc. He began to laugh half-hysterically.

Delia was staring at him, horror-struck. He saw she grasped the state of his emotions. She was worried, her hazel eyes full of fear because she understood.

"Please, Tom, it will be all right. Don't make that sound anymore."

His sister's sudden awareness of passing days and months, her anger, the Christforsaken cups of tea she brought the old woman—how much time had Delia been spending with the hag? Oh Jesus, he didn't know.

His brain reeled.

He was going to kill the fucking witch with his bare hands.

He grabbed the foul thing, ripped it from the child's arms. It was wet and slick between his hands, as greasy if it had been dipped in pitch.

"Tom, don't. Please don't." She hung on him, clawing.

He shook her off.

"Don't!"

He threw it into the fire and immediately the liquid burned bright with an oily evil flame. He seized the bellows, pumping wildly to fan the blaze, praying the heat would crack the rock. A sickening stench blew in on them.

Delia mewled, she crawled between his legs. On her hands and knees, she stretched forward to try and grab hold of it.

"No, no. It's from Granny Rose. From Granny, Tom. She told me Ellen had one and where to find it. At the old church. Please don't," she wailed. "I didn't even have to dig it out—it came to me!"

He kicked the leering gargoyle viciously with the sole of his heavy boot and shoved it back farther into the fire.

Delia ran screaming to the corner. She sagged down until she was sitting. She began rocking herself to and fro. "Oh, my baby's going to die." She held her stomach and cried out in pain.

The obscene carving went dead black. Tom piled more kindling on top of it, and saw the blaze leaping higher still. He watched the sparks fly up the kitchen chimney with more glee than he would have thought possible.

Her breath was coming very hard. Gasping for air, Delia clutched her small chest. Suddenly she vomited up a huge rolling spray of liquid and half digested food. She moaned.

Tom ran to her side. He knelt. Her skin was ice cold, her face was covered in sweat.

She sat up and spread her legs as wide apart as they would go. "It's pushing, pushing," she panted. "In me." She began to shriek.

He took her hand. "No, it's too soon, Delia, no."

"Oaannnnnh," she grunted, and her teeth were set on edge. He saw blood flow in fast pool underneath her. She vomited again, and he saw her eyes roll up in her head. Her mouth dragged down in a sharp spasm and she screamed in agony. Her hands flew to her chest.

"Delia. Delia." He cradled her on his lap.

"Meat, meat for the baby." Her hair was matted with sweat, her hand fumbled at her crotch.

He screamed, unable to help himself.

"Did you eat it? Answer me, oh mother of Christ, Delia answer me!" Her legs splayed wide and he felt the wet flow of her blood onto his trousers. Her body jerked, and she cried out again, her small hands pressing her heart.

"Gran says meat," she breathed. "Eat it for the baby. Hungry." The words were indistinct, slurred. Her lips formed a thin half smile. "Papa says getting fat. Waited till you went to wash—"

The potatoes, he thought, and clutched her small body to him. He buried his head against her. God, God, she'd eaten the meat from the poisoned stew.

Her eyes opened and she looked at him. She nodded, barely. "Yes." It took her a long time to say it.

He heard the sharp intake of breath, then her body stiffened. He watched until her eyes clouded over. She was gone.

He heard a light step and turned to look over his shoulder. Rose stood alongside the table, one misshapen hand curled around a small paring knife.

"An abortifacient. You don't know that word, do you boy? No. You wondered what could stop the baby, but you never heard those women in town say, did you? Oleander works on the heart," she said. The short blade gleamed between her fingers.

He kept his eye on the knife, her words swirled like oil in his mind.

"Knew it would kill a pig didn't you? But not how much would kill a man or a poor slow witted girl, either, huh, boy?"

She'd been inching toward him slowly; he realized her voice held him—as if he'd been paralyzed—to the spot.

"I'm going to have your manhood!" Rose cawed.

At the same instant, from three feet away he saw the knife glide out of her hand. The vision was quite clear, she hadn't thrown it; it floated toward him at the level of his eyes, the thin curve where it had been honed too often gleaming like a sickle.

Rose laughed. "Trophies. Life is all about getting trophies, boy. Think of it," she said, and the knife took a sudden dive downward like a kite dropped by the wind. "You'll never know a woman."

He watched the blade begin a slow windmill spin.

The door banged open, Rose started at the noise, and Tom heard the knife clatter against the floor.

"What've you done to Delia?" Cedric shrieked, running forward; then he sagged to his knees in front of the fireplace and began wringing his hands. "Oh, my book, my precious precious book."

Tom saw the old woman's eyes flick toward Cedric and he seized his chance. He hurled himself at her and knocked her down. He heard her head strike the floor with a hard dull thud. She was half-conscious, moaning. He would deal with her later, he got to his feet, scrabbled sideways and snatched up the heavy soup kettle, dumping it over on Cedric. Cedric began spluttering and screaming in a blind rage.

"Oh Christ, mother of the dear Christ, I can't see. I'm scalded!" His hands circled and flailed like wounded birds around his face.

Cedric tried to hoist himself up, he flung his hands wide trying to find the wall, a chair, the bench—something to guide him. Tom lifted the burning kettle. He ignored the hot searing pain in his hands and brought it down against Cedric's head as hard as he could. Cedric fell sprawling on his face in the puddling stew.

Then he fell on Rose. He got astride her chest, his knees clamping her bony form. He yanked her hair and banged her head as hard as he could against the floor. The sound of her head striking the boards urged him on. He kept at it until he felt her go limp. A thin line of blood ran from one ear to the hollow of her shoulder.

Her words cut through the haze of his shock.

You can light fires with your mind.

Maybe it was a trick, her last try to overpower him. He didn't know, didn't care. He sensed there would be danger if he hesitated or delayed.

Tom jerked open the cupboard drawer where there was a small supply of linens. He shook the kerosene from a lamp over the napkins and cloths and tossed them in the four corners of the room. He spread the rest of the reeking liquid over the floorboards and furniture, close to their bodies, away from the door. He would need a place to escape. The oily smell was sharp, his nose ran, his eyes blurred from the fumes.

Rose groaned.

"Your burning is my trophy," he whispered.

Tom grabbed the pothook and scattered the fire.

The instant it touched the kerosene, he heard it suck up the oxygen with a loud whump. The flames jumped in a high savage dance.

He slammed the kitchen door, and ran out of the house.

"I never went back to the house in Meath," Tom said. "Never even went to see what was left after the fire. Ashes, bones, charred timbers," he shrugged. "I don't really know if my father and grandmother died—not that it matters with Delia gone...and Ellie."

"Phew." Jack Cahill glanced down at the bottle that was nestled in the triangle of his crossed legs. "It's got the ancient mariner beat by a mile—course I was never one for poetry," he grinned. His gaze met Tom's. "If all you say is true, I'd give an eyeball to own one of them dollies, a sheila na gig—"

"No," Tom said, exhaling deeply. "No, you wouldn't—"

"Why the hell not?" Jack poured them both another round of gin.

"Look here," Tom said. He unfastened the flaps of a frayed tapestry carpet bag, and tilted the opening toward Jack.

Jack peered in, whistling. "Say, it's one of them things—where'd you get it?" He reached out, and Tom jerked the mouth of the bag away.

"Don't touch it." Tom shook his head. "It's the same one—"

"What? You said you burned it up—"

"I did; this wasn't in my pack when I got aboard the ship. I found it three days ago." He shivered looking at the fire-blackened toad woman, the moist inky slit in her vulva.

"Oh, your Granny's mophole," Jack flapped a hand at him. "C'mon, you spun a good one, I'll grant you that—but tell the truth now—you picked it up in one of those junk shops on the docks."

Tom stared at the older man and shook his head slowly. "Maybe Granny's not dead," he said. He shut the bag up and pushed it deeper into the shadowy hold. "This thing, it sucks from a man at the same time it makes him think he's getting what he wants or needs. My father thought so—but it was draining him—as if there was a spigot in his spine leaking and dribbling out his blood."

"Well I'd take a flyer at it—if I thought I'd get what I wanted—including some tasty young piece to wrap around my whanger."

"I think the old hag used it—and used my father and Delia and Ellen to make herself stronger. They got worn down, and she got wound up."

"Give it to me—I'll run Wall Street inside of a week."

"Do you always drink this much, Jack?"

"Huh? Ah hell, there's nothin' to do, crammed down here below decks. What are you saying, anyhow?"

Tom folded his hands quietly in his lap. "I think maybe it doesn't matter whether you touch it or not, I think it can get at you just being near it."

"It's stone, Tom. A dirt-covered stone that was carved into ugliness by old savage ladies back when every Brit was still howlin' at the moon."

Tom didn't answer. Sure it was only dead rock, an object, a symbol. But what it stood for was his grandmother's power—and that could reach across time and miles and distance.

Souls don't die, they go into the bodies of the living.

The sheila na gig witched into his pack was just a nasty little reminder of Rose's future intentions, he thought. She lied about needing a man to dig it up, what else had she kept from him? What more could she do?

Your manhood's my trophy, boy.

Jack seemed to read his mind. "If I were you, I'd forget all this." He waved an arm to include Ireland, his grandmother, the carving, "just put one foot in front of the other, and build yourself a new life, lad."

"After we dock tomorrow, I'm going down South somewhere," Tom said. "Virginia or the Carolinas...."

"Me, for New York." Jack grinned, held up his cup in salute and clinked it against Tom's.

"Maybe I'll go to school, change my name to Grainger or Garner or—"

"Granville," Jack put in, winking.

"Granville's good," Tom agreed, thinking and even if she won't let me go, maybe my children will have a chance— become lawyers, businessmen, doctors....

He saw Jack's eyes were riveted on the worn carpet bag.

Tom would've offered to give the obscene carving to the older man, and gladly—Jack was greedy for it, that was plain—but somehow he didn't think he'd have to. And Jack wouldn't steal it, Tom was sure. The sheila na gig wanted the older man now, too, he thought sadly. It would tap into him until the sap poured out of him like maple running in the spring. And his grandmother would live again.

Jack was hunched over, brooding, a silent bird of prey guarding its bloody kill.

And Tom knew when he left the ship, his carpet bag would be lighter by the weight of the stone.

AUTHOR'S NOTES & ACKNOWLEDGEMENTS

I wrote both these novellas after completing a trunk novel which I wrote just after finishing *The Gentling Box* while that book was out making the rounds and both that novel and I were in limbo. (Some years later *The Gentling Box* eventually won the Bram Stoker Award which meant that I could pretty much stop worrying that I'd never be published or win an award I really coveted.)

But, an interesting thing about both these stories is, not only did I think (hope, surmise, pray) they were much better than that nameless hag-ridden trunk novel, but I began to really enjoy writing again and found myself in love with voice and character and all those interesting flourishes and details that make a story worth telling to readers and to myself.

Since at that point, *The Gentling Box* was a no go, it was with trepidation that I asked my mother, who was not only erudite, but an excellent critic of my work, to read both novellas.

When she finished the first one some hours later, we sat down with a couple of glasses of wine and talked a long time about *Dissolution* and how I was influenced by *Ethan Frome*. I recounted how I was simply amazed that information I could not find for love or money on Google was instantly obtainable through the Brooklyn Public Library. I called them up because I needed to know where a person who was adjudged criminally insane in 1893 would be sent, and they had an answer for me in under a minute:

Matteawan State Hospital. The young man who answered the phone found an article from a contemporary newspaper about a fugitive from justice who was caught on a train in Florida and shipped back up north. A journey that perhaps wasn't so different from Stuart Granville's odyssey. My mother countered with a couple of stories of her own including the time she was in nursing school and a patient of hers who scarcely weighed 90 pounds soaking wet had managed, in an instant, to rip off her canvas and leather strait-jacket, whip it around in one deft arc, and catch my mother with the buckle-end in the throat; and how it took four big orderlies to pull the woman off my mother who was 17 at the time.

We said our good nights, and in the morning, I was in my office working on something or other when I heard weeping from my living room.

I'm pretty impervious to disturbances of the human variety when I'm writing, (although I do curse a hell of a lot when I hear chain saws and leaf blowers) but since I knew my mother was out there, I went to check.

"What's wrong?" I said.
She had a big box of Kleenex, the chubbiest of my three cats, and the telephone tucked among the down pillows of an antique love seat, and the pages of the manuscript of *The Sheila Na Gig* spread out on the space the cat wasn't occupying, the floor around her, and her knees.
My mother's eyes turned even greener whenever she cried and it was very obvious she'd been crying.
"What's wrong?" I asked again.
"Nothing, absolutely nothing."
"Then why are you crying."
"I can't help it," she said... it's so good and I'm so sad about what happens to Delia."

My mother wasn't all that much of a crier when it came to books or movies as I knew. In fact, for example, while *The Exorcist* literally scared the shit out of me and I had to sleep with the light on for months and I warned her not to watch it alone, she reported laughing throughout the entire film.

I can't tell you what it meant to me to have her say those words: "It's so good and I'm so sad about what happens to Delia." Up until that point, the closest I'd come to any kind of validation (aside from garnering a couple of agents who could not sell *The Gentling Box*) was having one of my professors in graduate school tell me I should write and, because my best friend Barbara McGill Grant knew I was madly in love with William Styron's work and she was an acquaintance of his, a signed copy of *A Tidewater Morning* with the inscription, "Best of luck in your literary endeavors."

When I saw my mother crying and she told me how much she loved this collection, it was *everything* to me. Sure, I'd cried when I wrote scenes in *Dissolution* and wept throughout the last 20 pages while madly typing out the last of *The Gentling Box*, but to actually see someone who was a pretty tough cookie and definitely not afraid to pan my writing, and really *was* a good literary critic moved to tears really affected me. It made me realize that my work did have a power of its own....

A year or so later when she was ill and not just visiting, but living at my house, she was on the phone with my nephew, John, when I got the news (via e mail) I'd just made my first professional sale for a short story and she excitedly told my nephew about it and recounted the entire plot of that particular tale. The instant she was off the phone, she threw her arms out for a hug and said, "I'm so proud of you."

You see, it didn't matter to her whether I wrote a book, or a couple of novellas, or a story, or whether the material got published or not. What mattered to her was that I kept on writing, and kept on trying, and kept on trying to move and engage her emotionally through *how* I wrote.

No writer can ask for or receive a greater gift, a higher accolade.

So, this collection comes to a public life with thanks and gratitude to my mother, Anne L. Mannetti, my nephew John Peter Mannetti, my best friend Barbara McGill Grant, and finally, to Dr. Steve Ross, another believer in my work—even through times when I doubted myself.

Two of you are gone now, but I sense your presence, always, in whatever I do and whatever I write.

I'd also like to thank Beth Blue, my superlative editor for *Deathwatch* who went over the manuscript in what has to be record time. She has a keen eye for those small gaffes and, manages to ferret them out and correct them accurately and (from the writer's perspective) painlessly.

I'm also truly grateful to the members of the HWA who nominated *Dissolution* for a Bram Stoker Award in 2011, Paul Leyden who's smitten with the novella, Glenn Chadbourne for his inimitable, haunting cover art for this edition, Elizabeth Massie for her introduction, my fearless agent, Cherry Weiner, and last—but certainly not least—my wonderful new publishers Bob and Jennifer Wilson of Nightscape Press.

Grazie.
Mille Grazie.

—Lisa Mannetti
December 9th, 2013

ABOUT THE AUTHOR

Lisa Mannetti's debut novel, *The Gentling Box*, garnered a Bram Stoker Award and she has since been nominated three times for the prestigious award in both the short and long fiction categories: Her story, "Everybody Wins," was made into a short film and her novella, "Dissolution," will soon be a feature-length film directed by Paul Leyden. Recent and upcoming short stories include, "Resurgam" in Zombies: More Recent Dead and "Almost Everybody Wins," in Insidious Assassins. Her work, including *The Gentling Box*, and "1925: A Fall River Halloween" has been translated into Italian.

She has also authored *The New Adventures of Tom Sawyer and Huck Finn*, two companion novellas in *Deathwatch*, a macabre gag book, *51 Fiendish Ways to Leave your Lover*, as well as non-fiction books, and numerous articles and short stories in newspapers, magazines and anthologies. Forthcoming works include additional short stories and a novella about Houdini, *The Box Jumper*. She is currently working on two paranormal novels, tentatively titled *Spy Glass Hill* and *The Everest Hauntings*.

Lisa lives in New York in the 100 year old house she originally grew up in.

Visit her author website: www.lisamannetti.com
Visit her virtual haunted house: www.thechanceryhouse.com